BRILLSTONE BREAK-IN

BRILLSTONE BREAK-IN

Florence Parry Heide
and Roxanne Heide

Cover and Frontispiece by Joe Krush

ALBERT WHITMAN & COMPANY, *Chicago*

TEXT © 1977 BY FLORENCE PARRY HEIDE AND ROXANNE HEIDE
ILLUSTRATIONS © 1977 BY ALBERT WHITMAN & COMPANY
PUBLISHED SIMULTANEOUSLY IN CANADA
BY GEORGE J. MCLEOD, LIMITED, TORONTO

Library of Congress Cataloging in Publication Data
Heide, Florence Parry.
  Brillstone break-in

  (A Pilot book)
  SUMMARY: Two teen-age neighbors in a city apartment
building become involved in the theft of money intended
as a bribe for a public official.
  [1. Mystery and detective stories. 2. City and
town life—Fiction] I. Heide, Roxanne, joint author.
II. Krush, Joe. III. Title
PZ7.H36Br   [Fic]   77-2220
ISBN 0-8075-0888-8

BRILLSTONE BREAK-IN

PEOPLE YOU'LL MEET
AT THE BRILLSTONE APARTMENTS
in the order they appear:

LOGAN FORREST, whose hobby is his old car. He and his mother, JENNY, have a seventh-floor apartment. Jenny Forrest works for an advertising agency.

LIZA WEBSTER, Logan's friend and neighbor, whose hobby is *not* old cars. She and her father, WEBB, live on the eighth floor. Webb is a free-lance writer.

LOUIE, daytime manager at the Brillstone Apartments.

CHAN, short for Eric Chandler, officer in charge of assigning contracts for a large housing development. He has a court apartment on the second floor.

KELI MORRISON, secretary and typist, presently working at home in her tenth-floor apartment. Her husband is Thomas Morrison.

MR. HOYT, a chess-playing tenant who lives on the second floor, across the court from Mr. Chandler.

MICHELE TRILLING, four-year-old for whom Liza sits. The Trillings have a fourth-floor apartment.

MRS. MERKLE, also called MERK, a housekeeper shared by a number of Brillstone tenants.

E. SIMMS and M. BOWERS, partners in a construction company.

Chapter One

A police siren screamed past Logan's old car.
Liza turned around to watch the flashing red light
as it disappeared around the corner.

"I wonder what that was all about," she said.
Her long hair swung as she turned back. "Maybe a
big robbery."

"Probably a rescue for a kitten that climbed too
high and can't get down," said Logan. "You let
your imagination run away with you."

Liza shifted the packages on her lap as Logan
drove carefully through the traffic. He slowed as he
neared a large U-shaped apartment building.
"Brillstone Apartments, here we come," he said,
pulling into the drive which skirted the building
and led to the garage entrance at the back.

"Home sweet home," said Liza. "Fifteen floors
of it."

"Listen," Logan commanded. "I think there's
something the matter with one of my spark plugs.
The engine sounds rough."

"Fascinating," sighed Liza. "You're the only friend I have who'd rather listen to a spark plug than to a human being."

"Cars are like people. You have to care about their insides. What shows isn't all that counts."

Liza raised her eyebrows. "You mean under all that rust beats a heart of gold? I have news for you. Cars aren't a bit like people."

She leaned forward. "Maybe you could drop me off at the front entrance. I hate that garage. It's an overgrown gloomy two-story basement."

"I agree. But you want to help me carry in all the stuff from our errands, don't you?"

"I'm all carried out," Liza complained, but she smiled. "All erranded out, all driven out, all garaged out."

"It will just take a couple of minutes if we both do it," Logan promised.

"Have I told you that you're a very stubborn person?" Liza asked, making a face.

"Sure. I'm almost beginning to believe it," Logan said cheerfully, turning the car into the garage. Just as he was easing into his parking space the car stalled.

"Not again!" Liza exclaimed. "If this car isn't stalling or smoking or making strange noises, then the doors won't open or the windows won't shut.

Why don't you just junk it and start over with a bike?"

"This car is a honey," Logan answered, patting the dashboard lovingly. "All it needs is a little body work, a little surgery, and tender loving care."

He started the car again and pulled into his space next to the ramp to the second level.

He jerked his door handle hard and got out of the car. A workman on the upper level of the garage was drilling a hole into the concrete wall. The noise echoed and re-echoed.

Liza gritted her teeth. "I hate this place. It's not only spooky, it's noisy."

"The real reason you don't like the garage is because you watched that late movie on TV last week, 'Murder in the Underground Garage,'" teased Logan. "I don't know how you stay awake for things like that."

"And I don't know how you sleep through things like that."

Suddenly the garage was plunged into almost total darkness. The sound of the drill stopped at the same time.

"Fuse," muttered Logan. "He'll fix it in a minute."

"That isn't soon enough," said Liza. "I'm heading for the elevator and sanity." She started to feel her way through the garage to the elevator door.

Without warning, she bumped squarely into someone. There was scarcely any light, but she dimly saw the man's face. His thin mouth turned down at the corners under his drooping mous - tache. A ragged scar pulled one of his eyes down, making him look frightening in the dark. Liza pulled away, her heart pounding.

The lights came on. The man was gone. The door to the stairway slowly swung shut.

"See, lights!" called Logan. "It was only a blown fuse." Liza glanced up the ramp. The work- man was closing the fuse box. Logan shouted up to him, "Guess that fuse box isn't too happy about your drill!"

The man laughed. "Maybe the sound gets on its nerves. It sure gets on mine!"

Logan caught up with Liza. "In the dark I ran into a horrible man with a scar," she told him.

"And I saw a great big snake with horrible fangs," said Logan.

"But I *did*," insisted Liza.

"No more television for you," Logan ordered.

Liza glanced at their errand list. "First stop, Louie's repaired and renewed shoes. I don't know how he wears them out so fast, just managing the place. Maybe he tap dances when he's all by himself.''

They took the elevator up to the lobby and walked over to the desk. Liza set her packages down on the floor. "We brought your shoes back, Louie. Ready on Monday, as promised," Logan said to a small balding man. Liza took the shoes out of the paper bag and held them up.

Louie's blue eyes twinkled at Logan and Liza as he took the shoes. "New heels, new soles, new laces, and a super polishing job. Are you sure these are my old shoes? They look like new.''

Liza nodded. "Thanks, crew," said Louie. "I appreciate you. You're always doing nice things for me. Don't you ever get tired of other people's errands?''

"You bet," said Logan.

"Tired of the errands, but not tired of the people," said Liza.

She looked up and smiled as a tall gray-haired man with a deep tan approached the lobby desk. His dark tie and gray suit made Logan and Liza feel sloppy in their blue jeans and old shirts. Chan always looks as though he's just finished a tennis match and a shower, Logan thought.

"Our paths cross again," said Chan, smiling. "You're on your way back from your usual errands, and I'm on my way out to my usual meet-ings."

"You're famous, Mr. Chandler," said Louie. "Here's your picture in this afternoon's paper." He held it up. There was a large picture of Chan. The headlines read:

HEAD TO MAKE DECISION THIS WEEK
Housing Contract To Be Awarded

Chan smiled and said, "All those pictures of me in the paper lately make me feel like a movie star instead of an overworked businessman."

"I read the magazine article Liza's father wrote about the big housing development," said Logan. "And how you have to choose which contractor will build it."

Chan nodded. "Webb is a good writer. All the facts are there." He glanced at his watch. "My life is one meeting after another these days. Morning meetings, afternoon meetings, after-dinner meet-ings. But this is the last week. By Thursday night the contract will be settled. I'll be ready for that spe-cial dinner your dad's concocting, Liza. But this is only Monday. Thursday seems years away."

"I've just about been living at Webb's while my mother's in Bermuda," said Logan. "I can vouch for his meals."

"I hope she'll be back in time for Thursday's dinner, Logan," said Chan. "A party isn't a party without Jenny Forrest."

"She'll be back," Logan assured him. "Webb is picking her up at the airport Thursday afternoon."

"You know how Dad loves airports," said Liza. "Besides, he's planning to write an article about this one next month."

Chan smiled and started to walk toward the swinging doors to the driveway. "Hope you'll both be at the dinner, too," he said over his shoulder. "A party isn't a party without you two, either, remember."

"I admit we're pretty good dishwashers," said Logan.

They watched as Chan climbed into a waiting taxi.

"He's a celebrity, all right," said Louie. "Picture in the newspaper and everything."

Suddenly Liza grabbed Logan's arm. "That's the man, the man I saw in the garage," she whispered.

Logan turned around. The man was bending over to look at a magazine on one of the coffee tables. It wasn't until he straightened up that Logan saw the scar.

The man walked toward them. His voice was low and seemed strained as he asked Louie, "Does every tenant have his own parking space in the garage?"

"Yes," said Louie. "It costs extra, though."

The man nodded and pulled at his drooping moustache. Then he started through the big double doors to the outside.

Louie watched him go. "I'll bet my new shoes that he didn't mean it when he said he was interested in renting one of the Brillstone apartments."

"What do you mean?" asked Logan, frowning.

"Well, he comes in here today and says he wants to look at some vacant apartments. Fine with me, I say, and I take my keys and show him around. Does he ask about the rent or anything? Nope. He just looks out the windows. Doesn't even take a peek at the stove and fridge. Doesn't even try to figure out where his furniture would go. So I ask you: does that man want to rent one of the apartments?"

Liza smiled triumphantly as they headed for the elevator with their packages and shopping bags. "See? There was a man with a scar. I wasn't imagining him, and I wasn't imagining that he was sneaking around, either. I'm sure he was up to something, lurking in that big old garage."

"He was just checking out the garage to see if he could park his car there if he moves into the Brillstone."

"He doesn't want to move in here. You heard what Louie said about him. He just used that as an excuse to look around. Maybe he's a spy."

"Or a mad bomber," teased Logan.

As the elevator door opened, Logan said, "Wait a second. I forgot Mr. Hoyt's mail. He gave me his mailbox key. He doesn't want to leave his apartment for a couple of days because of his cold."

"I'll hold the door," said Liza. Logan put the shopping bags down and dashed through the lobby to the mailboxes. They filled a wall, row on row, a box for each apartment.

Logan took out Mr. Hoyt's key and his own ring of keys. He pulled out the letters from Mr. Hoyt's box and a postcard from his own. He read it on the way back to the elevator.

"Hey, listen to this, Liza," he said as the elevator door closed on them. "It's from my travelling mother. 'Blazing beautiful blue skies and not a worry in the world except are you positive you're getting enough to eat? My love to you and to our fantastic upstairs neighbors, Webb and Liza. See you all on Thursday. Jenny, alias Your Devoted Mother.'"

Liza laughed. "I guess it's not hard to tell that Jenny is in the advertising business."

"She even won this trip to Bermuda with some ad she wrote this spring," said Logan.

The elevator purred to a stop and the door swished open. "First stop, tenth floor, stationery for Keli Morrison," announced Liza. "Actually," she said as they walked down the corridor with their packages, "it's not Keli's stationery, it's Dad's. But Keli's typing all the letters he dictated to her. She's way behind because she ran out of his stationery last week."

They walked down the corridor and knocked on Keli's door. A pert, curly-haired young woman answered. She wore large glasses that seemed to cover most of her face. The blue rims matched her dress. She beamed when she saw Logan and Liza.

"You did remember the stationery. I promised your dad I'll have all the letters he dictated typed by tomorrow morning." She reached for the box that Liza handed her. "I'm getting pretty good at listening and typing at the same time. If I keep improving, I'll be able to juggle three plates and balance a tray on my head, too."

They smiled at her, and she said, "Thanks again. I'd ask you in for a Coke, but I've got to get to work. Secretaries who work at home are still secretaries. Free-lance secretaries. I have to struggle to make myself keep office hours."

"I know how it is," said Logan. "I'm a free-lance mechanic and I've got to get to work on my car, too."

Keli pushed her red lips into a pout. "Somebody put a huge scratch on my car yesterday in the library parking lot. From the front to the back. An inch wide. And they didn't leave a note or anything."

"How mean," said Liza.

"I'm insured, but it's a headache," sighed Keli. "Tell your dad I'll have the rest of the letters typed first thing in the morning. I'll call when they're finished, okay?"

She closed the door and they started down the hall. "Mr. Hoyt's mail next, second floor."

"I feel as if half my life is spent in an elevator," said Logan. "A large box that goes up and down is not my idea of transportation."

"I suppose your idea of transportation is that rusty old heap you love so much," laughed Liza.

Logan shook his head. "My feet come first. Then my car."

"It's us, Mr. Hoyt," Liza called cheerfully as they knocked on his door.

A tall stooped man with rimless glasses greeted

them. His sparse hair was combed over his balding head. Binoculars hung from his neck.

"We brought your mail, Mr. Hoyt," said Logan.

"Oh, my mail. Thank you." He thumbed hurriedly through the letters.

Liza glanced at the binoculars. "How are the pigeons doing today, Mr. Hoyt?" she asked.

"They always keep me entertained. Never a dull moment. Better than television. No commercials." He patted the binoculars. "Want to take a look?"

"Later, thanks," said Liza. "We've got some more deliveries to make."

"I wonder what everybody here at Brillstone would do without you," said Mr. Hoyt. "Every apartment building should have an enterprising errand person."

"Errand people," Liza reminded him. "We're a team."

They started for the elevator. "Two more deliveries," said Liza, looking at her list. "Then we're through for the day."

"An errand person's day is never done," said Logan, pushing the elevator button.

A few minutes later the last package was delivered and they were walking along the hall to the Webster apartment. "Are you coming for dinner again tonight?" asked Liza. "Dad's fixing a super omelet and popovers."

"Not tonight. I've got my photography class Monday nights. But your dad's invited me for tomorrow for ham and scalloped potatoes. My favorite."

"Photography class, hm? I suppose you want to take before-and-after pictures of your car."

"Why not?" asked Logan. "Want to come?"

"It might be fun. But I promised Mrs. Trilling I'd stay with Michele tonight so they can catch an early movie."

Liza reached for the key to the Webster apartment. "Come on in for a snack, anyway. Dad's finishing his article on Egyptian mummies. We can at least have a Coke."

As they walked in, Logan noticed for the millionth time how different Liza's apartment was from his own. The layout was exactly the same as his mother's apartment directly below, but the two apartments were not alike at all. The furniture here was worn and old-fashioned. Oriental rugs covered the floors, and old paintings hung on the walls. The bright modern look and splashes of color which filled the Forrest apartment were missing here, but there was plenty of warmth.

Logan decided once again that he felt as much at home here in Liza and her father's apartment as he did downstairs.

"I see Mrs. Merkle was here," said Liza affectionately, glancing at a note fastened to the refrigerator door.

" 'I left you some cookies in the cookie jar,' " she read. " 'Chocolate chip. And I'll finish the ironing when I come back Friday.' "

"Good for Merk," said Logan appreciatively.

"I'll take some cookies down with me to Michele when I go to take care of her, and one for Mimzie."

"I thought Michele Trilling was an only child," said Logan.

"She is. But now she's got an imaginary friend, Mimzie. Mimzie has to do everything that Michele does. She plays all of our games. I set a place for her at the table, I tuck her in for a nap. Michele even has a separate piggy bank for Mimzie with her name on it."

"Ask her to start one for me," suggested Logan. "I need it."

Liza suddenly groaned.

"What's wrong?"

"All those errands, and I forgot the most important one. The eggs for Dad's omelet tonight."

Now Logan groaned. "Not another errand!"

"I'll just run down to the deli. No cars, no garages, no lurking men with scars for me." She ran to the door and opened it, then drew back. The man with the scar was coming toward her!

Seeing Liza in the open door, he stopped, then hurried past her to the elevator.

Liza shivered and closed the door. Leaning against it, she said, "I'll talk Dad into having leftovers. I'm allergic to errands." Then she told Logan about the man in the hall.

"He's just looking the place over," Logan said reassuringly. "He wants to check out the garage and the layout and the elevators to make sure this is the kind of building he wants. No crime in that."

"I know," sighed Liza. But privately she decided she'd keep her eyes open for the man with the scarred face. She didn't want to run into him again. Especially in a dark garage.

But the mysterious man was far from Liza's thoughts the next night, Tuesday, as she sat with Logan and Webb after dinner.

Logan stretched and said, "I've really got to go. It's late. Thanks again for the dinner, Webb. You're the best cook I know."

"You're just saying that because it's true," said Webb. "But you'd better not let Jenny hear you."

"Mom says herself you're the best cook in the world," answered Logan.

There was a knock at the door.

"I'll go Dad," said Liza.

She gasped when she opened the door and saw Chan. His face was ashen as he leaned against the doorway.

"Chan, what's wrong? What's happened?" she asked.

Webb and Logan were on their feet. He's been hurt, thought Logan quickly. Or he's had a terrible shock.

Chapter Two

Liza drew Mr. Chandler into the living room. He sank into a chair and put his head in his hands.

"What is it, Chan?" asked Webb, setting down his pipe.

"Something terrible." Chan's voice was a strangled whisper. "I had to come here." He looked around blankly. "I had to tell you."

Webb glanced at Liza and Logan and said, "Let's go into my study."

Chan shook his head. "The kids can hear this. Maybe they can help." His shoulders sagged. "No, no one can help."

He sighed and sank further into the chair.

"I'll fix some coffee," suggested Liza, moving towards the kitchen.

Chan raised his hand. "Please, nothing. Just let me talk this out. I've got to tell you. I've got to."

Webb sat on the arm of his chair, his favorite listening position. Liza sat on the floor, her knees drawn up under her chin, and Logan did the same.

"I've just been robbed," said Chan hollowly.

Liza and Logan glanced at each other.

"Robbed?" Webb frowned. "That's terrible, Chan. Have you made a list of what's missing? The police will want to know."

"Fifty thousand dollars," said Chan slowly.

Fifty thousand dollars! Logan drew in his breath. Was there that much money in the world?

"That was a lot of cash to be carrying," said Webb, frowning.

"I wasn't carrying it. It was taken from my apartment. I just discovered it. Just now, when I came in."

"You've called the police," Webb stated flatly.

"I can't let the police know about it," said Chan.

Logan frowned and glanced at Liza. Not go to the police—to report a theft of fifty thousand dollars? Something was wrong here.

"I know what you're all thinking," said Chan, echoing Logan's thoughts. "You're thinking that I must have done something wrong if I don't want to report that the money is missing."

"No one is saying that, Chan," protested Webb.

"I can't blame you for thinking it," said Chan. "But let me tell you about it. I don't know where to turn, I don't know what to think."

Chan took a deep breath and pulled his shoulders back. "You all know about the conferences I've been attending. Every day all day, luncheon meetings, dinner meetings, evening meetings. I'm trying to work out the contract on the huge housing complex that's going to be built on the south side of the city. The contract must be awarded Thursday. But you've read about this."

"And Dad's written a couple of articles about it," said Liza.

Chan went on. "I was called out of our meeting this afternoon. My secretary told me it was urgent. I left the conference room and answered the telephone at my desk."

He paused, frowning. "It was Simms. Simms, of Simms and Bowers."

Webb interrupted quietly. "Perhaps you'd better tell Logan and Liza who they are. If we're going to get the picture, we'll need the background and all the facts."

"Simms and Bowers are building contractors," Chan explained. "They want to do the work on the housing complex and gave us a bid. They are well known. Never any hanky-panky or cheating as far as anyone has ever known." He frowned. "As far as anyone's ever known," he repeated slowly, giving the words a new meaning.

No one spoke. They all hunched forward.

"As you know, I'm chief of a section on urban development. That means that I'm in a position to award the contract on this housing center. I'm the decider, so to speak. You understand?"

Logan and Liza nodded.

"Well, Simms and Bowers is one of seven firms trying to get the contract. The decision was to be made—is to be made—this week."

Chan paused, clasping and unclasping his hands.

Webb turned to Liza and Logan. "There's a lot of money in these big housing developments. The firm that gets this contract will be very fortunate—right, Chan?"

"Of course," Chan agreed. "They stand to make an enormous profit. Anyway, it was Simms on the telephone. He said that there was an urgent message waiting for me at my apartment. I asked him what it was, and he just said, 'It's important, you'll see.' And that was all. I went back to the conference. But then I began to wonder. An urgent message? And at my apartment? I've lived alone since Elizabeth died. There would be no one there to take a message. Simms must have left the message there himself."

Chan stared at his clasped hands. "I began to

worry. Could it be possible that Simms—and Bowers—were trying to bribe me? Had they left money at my apartment, thinking I would accept it and give them the contract?''

Webb rubbed his cold pipe against his cheek, his eyes thoughtful. "Anyone who knows you would know that bribing you would be impossible, Chan.''

"But everybody doesn't know me," answered Chan.

"What did you do then?" asked Liza.

"I decided I'd have to get to my apartment to see what Simms meant. I made an excuse. I said I'd forgotten to bring some important papers. I said I'd be right back. I grabbed a taxi and came here to Brillstone." He paused. "My Ford has been in for repairs for some days. I've been using taxis."

Chan rubbed his hands together over and over. "When I got to my apartment, a big green plant was standing in the middle of the living room. There was a card: 'From a Friend.' There had to be something more. Simms wouldn't have called me out of my conference just to tell me he'd sent a plant.''

"But how did the plant get into your apartment?" asked Liza.

"I have an arrangement with Louie," said

Chan. "He always puts any packages in my apartment instead of my having to pick them up in the receiving room. I expect he brought it in."

Chan took a deep breath. "Anyway, I looked at the plant, trying to figure out if there was a message of some kind. And sure enough, there was a small pot inside the larger pot. Between the two pots—under the smaller pot—was a package. And in it—money. There was a slip of paper: $50,000."

A siren wailed on the street below.

Chan lifted his head and looked around the room. "I was furious. I picked up the telephone to call Simms to tell him I was outraged, that I would report him to the police, and so on. But the answering service said that Mr. Simms and Mr. Bowers had left town. They couldn't be reached until the end of the week. I tried them at their home telephones. No answer."

He buried his head in his hands once again. "Then my telephone rang. It was the others at the conference. They needed me, there were urgent decisions to be made."

Liza shook her head. This couldn't be real.

"The money," Webb prompted.

"I put it into a bureau drawer, pulled some shirts over it. I didn't know what else to do. I'd figure something out after the conference."

"You couldn't call the police?" asked Webb, frowning.

Chan shook his head. "No. I couldn't. Of course I was not keeping the money. But I had to think it through. Simms had left the money as a bribe. I knew that. But how could I prove it?" He cleared his throat and continued. "I hailed another cab and went back to the conference. I was sure the money was safe where I had left it. After all, there was no way anyone could know where it was."

He drew a breath. "And when I returned to my apartment just now, I'd decided to call the police. I went to get the money—and it was gone! Gone. It's almost as if I dreamed the whole thing."

"But who knew the money was in your apartment?" asked Logan.

"No one could possibly have known. Except Simms. And Bowers. They would hardly steal it back!"

"Could they have told anyone?" asked Liza.

Chan shook his head. "Hardly. Bribery is a crime. They'd be fools to take anyone into their confidence. And they're not fools. Crooks, yes, I know that now. But not fools."

He ran his long fingers through his hair. "They expected me to be angry. That's why they left town.

They probably figured that when I cooled off I'd listen to reason. Their kind of reason—money. They thought I'd be tempted to keep it."

He stood up and started to pace nervously around the room.

"Who has a key to your apartment?" asked Logan.

Chan paused. "Louie has a passkey to all of the apartments, of course. Naturally, Mrs. Merkle, but we all know Mrs. Merkle."

He stopped and looked earnestly from one to the other. "And who could possibly have known that the money was there in my bureau drawer? Under some shirts?"

No one spoke for a moment.

"Was the window shade up in your bedroom when you hid the money?" asked Liza.

Chan frowned. "I don't remember. I know I didn't change it, whichever way it was. I do remember that I turned on the light." He shook his head. "But my apartment is on the second floor. No one could have seen in anyway, shade or no shade."

"Your bedroom faces the court," Logan reminded him.

Chan nodded. "I see what you mean. The windows of the Brillstone apartments on the other side of the court." He forced a smile. "But no one could have looked into my apartment unless they were very tall or unless of course they had binoculars."

Binoculars! Logan and Liza looked at each other. Mr. Hoyt? Of course not. Liza shook her head and Logan smiled. They seemed to be on the same wavelength. They always were.

"Mrs. Merkle might remember about the window shade. There was a note from her on my refrigerator door. She'd dropped off some clean shirts for me," Chan said.

"But even if someone could have seen into your apartment with binoculars, they'd have assumed you were just putting away your socks or something," said Liza. "Unless they knew what they were looking for."

"Look, Chan," said Webb, pointing at him with his pipestem. "This is serious business, and I suggest you call the police immediately."

Chan started to interrupt, and Webb held up his hand. "Of course I understand why you don't want the police in on this. It might look as if you had accepted the money. But I think you must call them anyway."

Chan shook his head. "I can't. I'd be ruined forever. Everyone would believe I had accepted money to do a favor. Of course, I _could_ just award the contract to someone else—Simms and Bowers must have thought they weren't in the running. But I'm afraid of what they might do. My life might even be endangered. If only I had the money—" He looked around.

Logan spoke quickly. "Is it all right if I check out your apartment, Chan? I might see something you missed. Something that would give us some clue."

"There's nothing there," objected Chan. "Nothing but that blasted plant. But of course you're welcome to look around. I'll come down with you."

"Maybe it's better if no one knows you've told us," said Logan. "I can slip down the stairs alone. No one will see me, no one will see us together."

Chan nodded and reached into his pocket. "My one and only key," he said. "That's why I don't understand—" He let the sentence hang in the air.

Logan took the key and started out of the apartment, stopping long enough to ask, "Where did you put the money? Which drawer of what bureau?"

"Bedroom bureau, third drawer down," said Chan. "Under my shirts, left-hand side."

Logan nodded. He let himself out of Webb's apartment and started for the stairway.

He ran down the steps, his rubber soles making no sound. When he got to the second floor, he paused and opened the door cautiously. No one was in the corridor. He tiptoed the few steps to Chan's apartment and let himself in.

Chapter Three

Logan looked around the living room. He'd been in Chan's apartment before, two or three times. It was like the Forrest and Webster apartments, but smaller. Large living room, dining alcove, bedroom, bathroom, kitchen. Shelves filled with books, tables piled with magazines and newspapers.

He saw the plant in the middle of the room right away. It was a large cut-leaf philodendron. There was a very big wooden planter and in that another, smaller pot, this one pottery. The small pot must have rested on the package of money.

Logan looked around thoughtfully. He walked into the bedroom.

The shade was drawn. Maybe the thief had pulled it down, Logan thought.

The bureau, third drawer down. Logan opened it and peered inside. Shirts neatly folded. It was under these shirts that Chan had hidden the money.

Someone must have seen him put it there.

Striding over to the window, Logan pulled up the drawn shade. Lights from the windows of the apartments across the way shone brightly. Logan leaned closer to the window. If he had binoculars, he could see into some of the other Brillstone apartments. Someone with binoculars could be spying on him right now!

Mr. Hoyt had binoculars, but he wasn't the type to steal. Neither was Louie, neither was Mrs. Merkle, both of whom had keys to Chan's apartment. Come to think of it, no one was the type.

The criminal type: Who fit the pattern? What kind of personality did a thief or a crook have? Logan shook his head. If every criminal went around with a sign around their necks: "Here I am. I did it," solving crimes would be a simple matter. But it just wasn't that way. The fact was that anyone could be a crook.

Anyone.

Logan pulled the shade down thoughtfully. They could find out which apartments had a good view of this bedroom. Maybe Mrs. Merkle would remember about the shade. Chan said she had stopped in and left a note and some shirts.

He heard a key turning in the lock. He started back to the living room. The door was just opening. "Chan, when you came back—" Logan started to say.

The door slammed shut.

Logan ran over and threw the door open. At the end of the corridor, the stairway door softly swung shut behind a dark figure. He ran over and flung it open. Someone was running up the stairs. Someone with rubber soles.

Not hesitating, Logan raced up the stairs, taking three steps at a time. Breathless, he reached the next landing. No one in sight. The door was closed. Had someone just slipped through? Or started up another flight of stairs? Was someone up at the next landing, listening and waiting?

Logan held his breath and listened. Nothing. He peered up, but there was no way he could see around the corner. He hesitated only a moment. Then he threw the door open. Glancing down the corridor, he saw the elevator door just closing. He ran toward it, but he was too late.

His eyes darted to the numbers which showed what floor the elevator was passing. It was on its way up. Whoever was in it could get off on any floor and walk up or down the stairs to any other floor. There was no way Logan could follow. He'd lost out. For good. The person would never come back. Logan silently blamed himself. He hurried up the stairs to Webb's apartment.

When Chan heard about the intruder, he frowned. "Someone trying a key in my door? You're sure?"

"I'm positive," said Logan. "Whoever it was opened the door and ran when he heard my voice. If I'd had my wits about me, I'd have kept quiet. I should have known it wasn't you—I had your only key. He'd have come on in and I'd have seen who it was."

Liza's eyes were troubled. "Maybe it's lucky you scared him off," she said quietly. "You might have—"

Chan interrupted. "Liza's right, Logan. You could have been in real danger. I shouldn't have involved any of you. I'm sorry. I've been thoughtless. This isn't your headache, it's mine."

"Nonsense, Chan," said Webb. "Problems are to solve, and friends are to help." He shook his head. "Although how we can help, I admit that I don't for the life of me know."

Suddenly the telephone rang shrilly. Liza jumped and then laughed self-consciously.

Webb frowned and reached impatiently for the telephone. "Webb here," he said, closing his eyes. That was one of his habits, thought Logan. Closing his eyes when he talked on the telephone.

Suddenly his eyes flew open and as he sat forward, listening intently, his eyes narrowed.

"Who are you?" he asked abruptly.

Logan could hear the sudden dial tone from where he sat. Whoever it was had hung up.

"What was that?" asked Liza, frowning.

"Oh, just a crank call," said Webb with a troubled frown.

"Tell me," demanded Chan, rising out of his chair, his jaw thrust out.

"Nothing, nothing, just a wrong number," Webb assured him, but Logan could see the anxiety in his face and hear it in his voice.

"What was it?" asked Chan, spacing the words.

"A man's voice," said Webb finally. "This is what he said: 'This is not your problem. I repeat, this is not your problem.' Then he hung up."

Liza gasped. "What does it mean?"

Chan interrupted, "It means that I have got you all in some kind of trouble. Whoever stole the money must be desperate, and desperate people do desperate things. That settles it. I'll call the police. You shouldn't be tangled up in this at all."

Chan stood up. "And I'll get Louie to change my lock tomorrow. Locking the barn door after the horse has been stolen, I guess." He walked to the door. "Thank you for listening. I somehow feel that telling you all about it has been a first step." He let himself out.

A first step, thought Logan. He wondered how many more steps there would be and where the steps would lead them.

He looked at Liza. She caught his eye and shivered. Then she must sense danger, too. Was someone watching? Waiting to see what they'd do?

"Chan was right, you know," said Webb. "Saying that desperate people do desperate things. I don't want you two involved in this in any way, hear?"

"Hear, hear," agreed Liza, smiling.

"Who could have taken the money?" asked Logan. "And who came when I was there? A second would-be thief?"

"Maybe whoever took the money in the first place developed a guilty conscience and was trying to return it," said Webb with a smile. "In any case, remember, you two stay out of it. It could be dangerous. Chan said he'd call the police. They'll handle it."

Logan stood up. "I'd better let you two catch some sleep," he said.

"Speak for yourself," said Liza. "You're the one who's sleepy. Dad and I are good for another couple of hours."

"Night owls," muttered Logan.

"We admit it," said Liza. "Be careful," she warned as he started out the door. "Maybe someone is waiting and watching on the stairs. Remember that man with the scar."

Logan nodded seriously. There might not be a man with a scar lurking in the hall, but the evening had already been full of strange events. "I'll be careful," he promised Liza and her father.

He stepped into the corridor and listened. No one. Was someone waiting on the landing below? Well, they'd better get out of his way then. He strode down the corridor and opened the door to the stairway. He'd ask Louie about who delivered the plant when he was back on duty in the morning.

Logan whistled and started down the stairs. Walking down the hall to his apartment, he saw it. A plain envelope propped against his apartment door. No one was in sight. Everything was silent. He reached for the envelope. No name was on it, but Logan was sure it was intended for him.

For a moment he fumbled with his key before he unlocked the door and shut it behind him. Then he tore open the envelope and held the message under a lamp. It was on a plain card and read KEEP OUT in large letters.

Logan knew what it meant. Keep out of this business with Chan. A warning. Like *No Trespassing* or *Beware of Dog, Danger.*

Logan stared at the card. He was not going to let this scare him off. He reached for the telephone to call Liza. Then he hesitated and put the phone back on its cradle. No sense in worrying her.

Chapter Four

Logan spent a restless night, and then over-slept. He woke thinking about the message left for him last night: KEEP OUT. The message, and the phone call to Webb: THIS IS NOT YOUR PROBLEM. Who could have known Chan had come to them? The person at Chan's door when Logan was there?

He frowned and reached for the telephone and dialed Chan's number. Chan would want to know about the KEEP OUT sign. The police should have all the facts. Had Chan called the police? Or had he changed his mind?

Mrs. Merkle answered the telephone. "Mr. Chandler's residence," she said in her special formal voice.

"Hey, Merk, it's me, Logan."

"Oh, hey, Logan, it's me, Merk. What can you do for me today? If you're trying to get Mr. Chandler, he's left already in a taxi."

Logan wondered if Chan had called the police. Again he thought of the warnings, and again he frowned.

"How about answering me a question, Merk?" asked Logan.

"If I answer right, do I get a prize?"

"You bet," promised Logan. "Here's the question. Do you remember when you took the shirts into Mr. Chandler's apartment yesterday afternoon?"

"Yes, I remember. Now do I get the prize?"

"Almost," answered Logan. "Do you remember whether the shade in the bedroom was up?"

"Yes, I remember that, too," said Mrs. Merkle. "And now here's a question for you: Is that all you want?"

Logan sighed. He should be used to Merk after all these years.

"I'll ask the question a different way. Was the shade down in the bedroom?"

"Negatory," said Mrs. Merkle. "That means no. That means that the shade was up. The shade was up, and the sun was coming in. I could see the window needed washing and I'm going to wash it as soon as I can get you off the phone. Do I get my prize?"

"One fat doughnut fresh from the bakery the next time you come," Logan promised.

"The kind filled with jelly," announced Mrs. Merkle, hanging up.

Logan rubbed his chin. Someone could have been watching Chan's window from across the way. Someone with binoculars could have seen him when he hid the money in the drawer. And could have seen him leaving again, in the taxi.

Someone who lived in the Brillstone Apartments? Or someone who was hiding there?

He thought suddenly of the man with the scar.

Logan showered and dressed in a hurry. He'd go down and talk to Louie.

Before he left, he dialed Webb and Liza's number. "Mmph," said a sleepy voice.

"And a cheery Wednesday morning to you, too, Liza," said Logan. "I have news for you."

"And I have news for you," yawned Liza. "I'm not awake yet."

"That's news? Listen. Chan's shade was up. Someone could have used Mr. Hoyt's binoculars to see Chan hiding the money."

"At least we don't have to look for someone with X ray eyes," said Liza. "Or a giant."

"I'll be up in ten minutes. That should give you time to get your brain working."

"You dreamer," murmured Liza. "I'm not a morning person."

"I've noticed," said Logan. "Got any fresh coffee cake up there? With Mom gone this week, I keep forgetting to get any food in the apartment.''

"I've noticed," said Liza.

"Rise and shine, morning glory, and I'll see you for breakfast," said Logan.

"Breakfast, you said. I'll be glad when Jenny comes back tomorrow.''

Logan grinned and hung up.

He ran down the stairs to the lobby. Louie was sitting on a bench, helping the Bonson boy tie his shoes.

"And there you go," said Louie. "Mind you keep those shoes tied. Tripping on your shoelaces is a good way to knock your teeth out.''

The boy ran off toward the elevator.

"Next!" said Logan, and Louie looked up and smiled. Logan leaned over so no one could hear. "A quick question, Louie: Did someone bring a big plant over for Mr. Chandler yesterday when you were here?''

"You bet," said Louie, nodding vigorously. "Just before I left. A little round guy with a smile as wide as he was. And a gold tooth set smack in the middle of the smile. He carried a cane, too. Didn't use it, but carried it.''

Louie rubbed his forehead with a stubby finger. "You'd have thought it was a million dollars he was bringing, not just a plant. He was so fussy. He insisted I take it right up to Mr. Chandler's apartment that very second. I almost thought he was going to ride up in the elevator with me. Acted like he didn't trust me."

Logan fingered the keys in his pocket. He'd forgotten to ask Chan what Simms and Bowers looked like. The man with the plant, could it have been Simms or Bowers?

"Did anyone see you with the man and the plant?" asked Logan.

Louie puzzled a moment. "Lots of people could have seen us. All the tenants were just getting home from work and all that. I can't say which ones, though. I just can't remember." He paused. "Anything wrong?"

"Nothing," Logan assured him. "But don't say anything to anyone about my asking, okay? That's just between you and me."

"You bet," said Louie. "You kids are always up to something."

Logan winked. It was all right if Louie didn't take him seriously. "One more thing. Do you remember anything else about the man with the scar who wanted to rent an apartment?"

Louie shook his head. "Just what I told you before. Said he wanted to rent one of the apartments here. He didn't seem interested. Just nosy."

Logan walked over to the stairway, thinking. He whistled all the way up to the eighth floor, and he was still whistling when he knocked at the door of Webb's apartment.

"I heard you coming all the way," said Liza, opening the door. "You'd make a rotten private eye. You whistle too loud."

"I didn't even know I was whistling," said Logan.

"Talk about being asleep when you're awake," said Liza.

Webb was there, too, sitting at the table in the breakfast nook. "Try my special coffee cake," he said.

"You needn't urge him, Dad," said Liza. "He's already drooling."

Logan sat at the table with Webb and Liza.

"About last night—" he started to say.

Webb interrupted. "Logan, I've just talked to Liza about it. We've got to stay out of this. Chan told us he'd be in touch with the police. There's nothing more we can do. Or at least nothing more we should do." He glanced at Liza with concern. "I don't want you kids mixed up in this. It's a matter for the police."

Logan nodded. "Okay, Webb. But we've got to do what we can. We're on the inside. We live here.

We know the people. We can help."

Webb sipped his coffee. "I repeat, this is not our problem," he said finally.

"You didn't recognize the voice on the phone?" asked Liza.

Webb shook his head thoughtfully. "I've never heard that voice. I remember voices. No, it was a stranger to me. He must have known that Chan would come to me. To us. Anyone who read that article I wrote would gather that we were friends."

"What do Simms and Bowers look like, do you know?" asked Logan.

"I know because I talked with them when I was writing that piece on the new building complex. That's also how I know it wasn't either of them on the phone last night."

Webb rubbed the bowl of his unlit pipe thoughtfully. "Simms is a round, bald little man. He seems to like old-fashioned clothing—I mean when's the last time you've seen a pair of spats? Never, I guess. He carries a cane which he doesn't need, at least he doesn't need it for walking. Carries it for looks or maybe to point with."

A cane! thought Logan. Then the man with the plant *had* been Simms.

"Maybe the cane has a concealed weapon," said Liza.

"That's what you get for watching so much television," said Logan.

"Well, you never know," said Liza defensively.

"What else about Simms?" asked Logan.

"His smile. He smiles constantly, showing off a gold tooth. A high-pitched voice. Round eyes. No glasses."

"He brought the plant," Logan announced. "Louie said he acted nervous about the whole thing."

"No wonder, with fifty thousand dollars sitting in that pot," said Liza before her father could speak.

"What about Bowers?" asked Logan. "What does he look like?"

Webb considered. "Almost the opposite of Simms. Tall and thin and dark. He has a long moustache which he pulls, maybe to make it grow longer. Although who knows, he may only be trying to pull it off." Glancing at Liza, Webb added, "Or maybe he has a long sharp knife hidden in it." Then he turned back to Logan. "A scar over his eye pulls the eye a bit awry."

"That's the man we saw in the garage!" Liza exclaimed. Logan nodded, frowning, then he and Liza told Webb about their Monday adventure.

"And the man with the scar asked Louie to

show him a couple of empty apartments," said Liza. "Only he didn't even ask what the rent was."

"So the man with the scar—Bowers—must have been looking around the Brillstone Apartments. Maybe he was trying to figure out how he and Simms could leave the money for Chan," Logan finished.

"I think that could be right," said Webb, rubbing his empty pipe. "Let's consider this: When Bowers came over to Brillstone on Monday, it was to look around. He pretended to Louie that he was interested in renting an apartment. But he just wanted to find out how to get into Chan's apartment to leave the money. Yes, kids, it's possible."

Liza broke in. "And I know why he was in the garage. He must have been looking for Chan's car! Maybe so he and Simms could put the money in it. It wasn't there, so they had to figure out something else. The plant."

"That would explain Bowers lurking around on Monday," said Logan. "But then who stole the money Tuesday?"

Webb rubbed his chin. "It was not Bowers or Simms on the telephone last night." He glanced up. "Stay clear of this, kids," he urged. "Fifty thousand dollars is a lot of money. Men have killed for less."

Logan fingered the keys in his pocket. He said, "We know it was Simms who left the plant in Chan's apartment. What if it was Bowers who stole it?"

Liza and Webb looked at him. "Possible," said Webb slowly. "If he hadn't really approved of the bribe. Or if they'd changed their minds and decided it was too risky—"

"But then who was it who tried to get into Chan's apartment later after the money was stolen, when Logan was there last night?" asked Liza. "And who was it who called to warn you to stay away?"

Logan added to himself, "And left me the KEEP OUT sign?"

"Now, let's have no more," said Webb. "If the police want to ask you questions, they will. Have another piece of coffee cake."

"You talked me into it," said Logan, reaching for it. "I need some for extra energy to work on my car. I'm going to make it perfect."

"You need more than energy for that," said Liza. "You need a magic wand."

"Abracadabra!" said Logan, waving the coffee cake in the air.

"Now you've done it. You've probably turned that old car into a pumpkin," said Liza.

"In which case, I'll make some pumpkin pie," laughed Webb.

The telephone interrupted their talk.

"I'll take it, Dad," said Liza quickly. She picked up the telephone. It was Keli.

"Sure, Keli," said Liza. "I'll tell him. And Logan and I will be there at two to get everything. I'll be staying with little Michele Trilling till then." She hung up.

"Keli said to tell you she's late with your letters and manuscript, Dad, but she'll have them done by two o'clock. Logan and I can stop by to pick up everything. We've got a new batch of errands to do this afternoon anyway."

"I never thought I'd grow up to be an errand boy," groaned Logan.

Webb stood up and stretched. "Off to my study, with one hot cup of coffee and one cold pipe. And forget this whole thing about the stolen money."

"What money?" asked Liza. Webb smiled at her affectionately and carried his coffee into the study.

"One last piece of coffee cake and I'm on my way down to the garage," said Logan. "I've got to regap my spark plugs."

"Whatever that means," said Liza. "You spend half your life in that garage. You might as well be a car."

"I can think of worse fates," said Logan.

Liza glanced at her watch. "I've got to go to Trillings to be with Michele. Mrs. Trilling works at the hospital Wednesday mornings." She paused. "On my way, I'll stop at Mr. Hoyt's and check out his binoculars. Just to see whether someone could have looked into Chan's apartment and seen him hiding the money in the bureau." She hesitated and added quickly, "Not that it could be Mr. Hoyt. But someone could have come in and used his binoculars last night. I can find that out. Dad won't mind."

"Okay," said Logan, standing up. "Meet you back here at two. I'll work on my car while you're baby-sitting."

"It isn't baby-sitting, it's child care," corrected Liza.

"Okay. I'll be restructuring my automobile while you're child caring. I'll just take one little piece of coffee cake with me."

"And I'll take some to Mr. Hoyt. It will give me an excuse to stop in."

Liza rang Mr. Hoyt's bell and immediately heard him bustling about inside. "Who is it?" he asked through the door.

"It's me, Liza. Thought you might like some coffee cake."

"Very kind of you—and your father," Mr. Hoyt said when Liza had settled herself in a chair.

After a few moments of silence, Liza asked, "Do you mind if I take a quick look at your birds—through the binoculars?"

"No, of course not, my child. But put the strap around your neck. I'd be lost if they happened to fall."

Liza gazed out the window, across the courtyard. She gasped as she saw Mrs. Merkle cleaning Chan's window. Why, she could see right into the room!

Mr. Hoyt quickly took the binoculars from Liza. "No, no! The birds are over there. Here, let me show you."

But Liza had seen enough, and she went back and sat down.

"What do you do evenings, Mr. Hoyt?" Liza asked casually.

"Lots of things. I read. I watch television, but not if it's boring. I talk back at the commercials. And I play a game of chess with a friend." Mr. Hoyt patted his thin hair. "Maybe that kind of evening sounds dull to you young people, but actually it's heaven." He raised his eyebrows. "Sometimes I put my slippers on right after supper, too. And that's heaven."

Liza smiled at him and walked over to the chess-board that was always set up on the table in front of the window. "It looks as if you're in the middle of a great chess game right now," she said.

Mr. Hoyt nodded. "We played for two hours last night."

Liza's heart beat faster. So someone had been sitting at this table last night! She tried to make her voice sound natural. "An old friend, Mr. Hoyt?"

"You bet," said Mr. Hoyt, blinking at Liza. "In fact, he's older than I am."

The telephone rang. "Excuse me," said Mr. Hoyt. "I believe that's the call I've been waiting for. My old friend. We play chess on the telephone. He must have figured out his next move."

Mr. Hoyt listened a moment, lost in thought. Then, without hanging up the phone, he walked over to the chess table and moved one of the pieces. "I don't like this," he muttered, "I don't like this move at all."

Liza let herself out and walked thoughtfully to the elevators. Mr. Hoyt and his friend played on the telephone. There was no one to look through the binoculars. No one but Mr. Hoyt himself.

Liza took the elevator to Mrs. Trilling's floor and walked down the corridor. "No time to think about Mr. Hoyt now," Liza said to herself.

Mrs. Trilling was waiting and opened the door before Liza had time to knock. "So glad you're here, dear. I'm really in a rush."

Leaning down to give Michele a quick kiss goodbye, Mrs. Trilling suddenly asked, "Why aren't you wearing your nice new shoes?"

"Mimzie wanted to wear them," said Michele.

Mrs. Trilling glanced up at Liza and winked. "I see. Well, have a good time, you two. I mean, you three. Liza, I'll be back at one. Fix yourselves some lunch."

"Mimzie wants hot dogs today," said Michele.

"And hot dogs it will be," Liza told her. "Look, I've brought a new book to read." Liza sat on the couch.

"You're sitting on Mimzie," objected Michele. Liza smiled and moved over. "Excuse me, Mimzie," she said solemnly. Since she couldn't see Mimzie, it was hard to keep thinking of her as a person. But she'd have to try, to keep Michele happy.

Chapter Five

Logan glanced at his watch as he strode through the lobby on his way to meet Liza. Nearly two. They had to be at Keli's by two.

He smiled as Louie waved and walked over to him. "Can't stop for a visit, Louie. I've got to pick up something from Keli Morrison. And first I have to pick up Liza."

"You sound pretty organized," Louie commented. "What's up with Keli Morrison, anyway? She was down here an hour ago all dressed up and made up as if she was ready to have her picture taken." He nodded and added, "Really looked special, and she was pretty excited, too."

"You've got me," shrugged Logan, his hand on the stairway door. A few minutes later he and Liza were outside Keli's door. At their first knock, Keli threw the door open.

Now Logan knew what Louie meant about Keli's being all dressed up. She was wearing a lavender pants suit which matched the frames of her enormous glasses. Lavender earrings dangled from her ears, and even her shoes were the same color.

"Oh, I'm so glad you came!" Keli cried, her round eyes bright behind her glasses. "I need you so much! Come on in. Forgive the mess."

The apartment was a mess, thought Logan. Quite unlike the usual neat Keli. Luncheon dishes weren't yet cleared away. The table had been set for two, so Keli must have had a guest. A man's coat was flung over a chair, and a pair of men's shoes were at the end of the couch. Newspapers and sheets of yellow lined paper were everywhere.

"This apartment looks like my mind, all scrambled up," Keli apologized as Liza looked around. "I haven't even picked up the lunch dishes." She lifted a plate, then stopped and turned around. "I'm so disorganized I haven't even told you why I need you. It's a surprise! Thomas is back!"

"Thomas?" asked Liza, trying to make some sense out of what Keli was saying. Had Keli ever mentioned someone named Thomas before?

As if reading Liza's thoughts, Keli rushed on. "That crazy lovable husband of mine. He came in yesterday afternoon, weeks before I expected him. He was all excited and nervous, like a whirlwind really." She nodded toward the closed bedroom door. "You could have knocked me over with a feather, a small one."

"I guess I forgot you were married," Liza said quickly.

"Me, too," Logan added.

Keli laughed. "It's all right! I hardly know myself, half the time. He's the most coming-and-going husband a girl could have." She sighed and then brightened. "But he's worth it. He's the greatest guy in the world! I'm dying to have you meet him. You'll see for yourself. Just a sec. I'll get him. And then—oh, you wouldn't mind too much doing one teeny errand for me? I almost forgot."

"Not a bit," said Logan.

"I'll get Thomas first," said Keli, smiling as she opened the door to the bedroom. They could hear a man's voice, then Keli's. In a moment she came out. "All right, all right," she called back, blinking.

Liza raised her eyebrows.

The man's voice was nasal. "I need one hundred fifty by Thursday. I do mean one hundred and fifty, and I do mean Thursday."

"Don't worry, Thomas," said Keli. "Oh, here, I'll look up Argonne's number for you—" She started back into the bedroom again. Logan and Liza exchanged glances.

Keli was laughing gaily as she returned to the living room and shut the door. "The poor lamb," she said. She bit her lower lip. "He's really working too hard for his own good. He's resting now, and then he's got some more phone calls to make. Then he's going to dictate a couple more letters for me to type up and—oh, I forgot, the errand. Maybe you could mail a couple of his things for me. I'd do it, but I've got to type the letters for him he's going to dictate. Do you mind terribly?"

"Of course not," said Liza quickly. "We'll be glad to mail them."

"They're right here," said Keli, looking around the cluttered living room. From the heap of papers on the couch she drew three big brown envelopes. "I don't know how much it will be," she said, fumbling in her oversized purse.

"We'll let you know," promised Logan.

"And I'll need more stamps," she said. "I'll write it all down." She took a pencil from the desk and then leaned over the wastebasket and pulled out an envelope. She wrote hastily on the back. "Tell your dad I'm terribly sorry, but his things aren't quite ready, Liza. I know he'll understand when he hears about Thomas."

"It's fine," said Liza reassuringly. "He's almost too busy today to sign the letters anyway."

"I really appreciate all this, kids," said Keli earnestly. "I've just got to help Thomas. It's not as if he comes all the time, you know. Our times together are so special."

"We'll be getting along, Keli," said Liza quickly. "We'll bring your stamps back later."

"You can meet Thomas then," said Keli with an eager smile. "You'll love him. There's nobody else like him. He's just a big kid. Know what he did? He vanished with my car yesterday afternoon. Just took the keys from my purse and vanished! I didn't care, but I just wish he'd let me know. Of course it was all right—I wasn't going anywhere."

An open briefcase was on the floor next to the couch, and Keli stopped to pick it up. "Business, business, with him it's all business."

Logan glanced at the briefcase. "T.O.M. for Tom, or T.O.M. for Thomas O. Morrison?" he asked.

Keli cocked her head and looked at the initials. "Thomas Otto Morrison. He always gets things monogrammed that way so people he meets on the road will remember his name is Tom. He never likes anyone but me to call him Thomas or Mister Morrison. Just Tom."

She set the briefcase on the couch.

"We'll mail the letters," said Liza, pulling at

Logan's arm. As soon as they were in the elevator, she said, "Why do women marry men who are gone all the time? And besides, I bet she supports him."

"That would be just as fair as his supporting her, wouldn't it?" asked Logan.

"Well, I'm not going to like him one bit," Liza predicted darkly.

"We'll see," said Logan. "You can't judge a person by hearing his voice once."

"Or the mess he makes, I suppose," said Liza.

"You're just spoiled because the men in your life are so neat," teased Logan.

"Besides, he pushes Keli around."

Logan glanced at the three manila envelopes in his hand. They were addressed in a sprawling scrawl to three different people at three different post office boxes. General Delivery. Bruce Garr, Fred Lennox, Max Danners. The return address was simply Thomas Morrison, General Delivery, Indianapolis, Indiana. He frowned. That didn't sound very businesslike. Keli's husband wasn't any of their concern, but—

"Our usual system," Logan announced as he pulled up at the post office substation. "I'll drive around the block while you run in."

"I don't know how anyone can do errands alone," said Liza.

In a few minutes Liza climbed back into the car. "I think there's something fishy about Keli's husband," she said. "Using a post office address in another city as his return address. It just doesn't sound right."

She glanced at the envelope on which Keli had written the list of stamps. Idly she turned it over. It was addressed in Keli's tiny cramped handwriting to Thomas, at a street address in Portland, Maine.

"She must have been writing to him when he showed up," she said. "That man wanders all over the map. Suddenly appearing out of the blue Tuesday. Taking her car without telling her. And the way he talks to her."

"I wonder what he does?" said Logan, pulling into the traffic. "All that moving about."

"It can't be honest," complained Liza.

"There's no crime in moving around a lot," said Logan.

"It's a crime to have a nice wife like Keli and never be home," insisted Liza.

"How many more errands?" asked Logan, braking to avoid a boy who had started to cross against the light.

Liza glanced at the list. "Five."

"In this traffic, we'd save time walking," he grumbled.

By the time they drove back to the Brillstone garage it was after four o'clock.

"Let's grab a bite at your apartment," suggested Logan. "Our refrigerator is empty, our cupboards are bare, and I'm starving."

"And what else is new?" laughed Liza. "Let's drop everything off and we'll raid our refrigerator."

"I was hoping you'd suggest that," said Logan. "That baked ham we just bought looked pretty good. And the Swiss cheese and—"

"And then you'll still be hungry when suppertime rolls around," Liza interrupted.

In a few minutes they were at Keli's door with the stamps. Logan set the bag of groceries on the floor and knocked.

"Stamps for the lady," he announced as Keli opened the door.

She had changed into a long green dress. The rims of her enormous glasses were green, too. Liza wondered how many pairs of glasses Keli owned.

"You're wonderful people," Keli told them. "I don't know what I'd ever do without you. My own errands, I guess. How much do I owe you?"

Liza handed her the receipt and Keli walked over to the desk to get her purse.

The dining room table in the alcove was set for

two, with flowers, candles, and wine glasses.

"We're having a special celebration dinner tonight," confided Keli. "It's almost our first anniversary, so I'm having all his favorite things. I had some steaks in the freezer, and when he went out to meet someone for a few minutes, I ran over to the deli and got all kinds of goodies."

The apartment was tidy again. "It won't last," thought Logan. "Not with Thomas around."

"He's in the shower right now," said Keli. She clapped her hand to her mouth. "The sauce! I hope I haven't let it cook too long!" She dashed out to the kitchen. She stirred rapidly and lifted a saucepan from the burner. "I guess I'm flustered," she confessed. "I'm so excited having him home."

"We'll leave now. Have a good time," Liza said, edging toward the door.

"Be sure to stop in the morning. You've got to meet him," urged Keli, tasting the sauce.

"We will," Logan told her.

"Is this Dad's envelope on the desk?" called Liza as they walked through the living room to the door.

"Yep," said Keli from the kitchen. "I haven't done all the letters, but I will in the morning. There are only about three left to go. I did finish the manuscript."

"That's the most important thing, anyway," Liza assured her, picking up the large manila envelope from the desk and slipping it under her arm.

As they walked back into Webb's apartment Logan announced, "And now for that snack."

Liza took the manila envelope into her father's study. She began to empty the contents. Then she frowned. She'd picked up the wrong envelope. Sighing, she put everything back and walked into the kitchen. "I've got the wrong stuff," she told Logan. "I'll just run this down to Keli's."

"If she's interrupted one more time, she'll burn that sauce," said Logan. "Let's do it later."

"Okay," agreed Liza. "Dad's not going to need his things tonight." She whistled as they unpacked the groceries.

There were two notes on the refrigerator door from Mrs. Merkle. One read, "I made some nice cheese dip for Mr. Chandler and put some in your refrigerator. Try it."

The other read, "Tell Mr. Chandler when you see him he better pay yesterday's parking ticket or they'll charge him double."

Liza smiled. "Mrs. Merkle is one-in-a-million. How about some crackers and Mrs. Merkle's cheese dip as a starter?"

"As a starter," said Logan.

Liza started to open the refrigerator door. "Wait a minute!" she said slowly. "How did Chan get a parking ticket yesterday afternoon? His car's been in for repairs. He's been taking taxis."

She handed the note to Logan and he read it, frowning.

"He was in meetings all day yesterday," said Liza. "The only time he left was to come back in a taxi to his apartment. To see what Simms had been talking about that was so important."

She looked up at Logan, her eyes troubled. "He wouldn't have lied to us about his car," she stated flatly. "Or about anything else."

"Of course not," Logan said quickly. "But what about a parking ticket for Tuesday afternoon?"

"Maybe Merk got things mixed up," said Liza. "Let's call her." She hurried into the living room, then paused, her hand on the telephone.

"She works for Chan Wednesday mornings, but—"

Logan joined her at the desk. "She always writes her own number and her schedule in all our telephone books." He flipped open the phone book. In her careful handwriting, Mrs. Merkle had written her own number, the number of her sister, and her schedule at Brillstone.

"Wednesday morning, Mr. Chandler. Wednesday afternoon, Mr. Hoyt," Logan read aloud. "Wonder if she's still at Mr. Hoyt's?"

"Let's give it a try," said Liza, picking up the telephone.

"Busy," Liza said in a moment. "I'll bet he's still playing telephone chess with his mysterious friend. It's hard to believe he'd spend that much time on a game. Come on. We'll just run down."

They rang the doorbell and Mr. Hoyt answered.

"Is Mrs. Merkle still here working?" Liza asked.

"No," said Mr. Hoyt. "She's still here, but she's not working. She's just looking through my binoculars at the pigeons. But do come in."

They could see Mrs. Merkle gazing through the binoculars. In a moment she put them down. "My, what a surprise to see you two here. Did you run out of cheese dip already?"

Before Logan could launch himself into his favorite subject, Liza asked about Chan's parking ticket.

"The police have a new system," said Mrs. Merkle. "And a new motto. 'Pay in a couple or you'll pay double.' It's like a poem."

"But Mr. Chandler's car has been in the garage all week," said Liza. "He couldn't get a parking ticket."

"All I know is what I see," said Mrs. Merkle. "And that parking ticket was for yesterday afternoon, and it was right there in his apartment. He probably forgot about it with all his meetings. That's why I told you about it. If any of you see him you can remind him. Otherwise he pays double. And in three days, triple. And so it goes till they get your last dollar."

Liza thought quickly. "Where's the parking ticket now?"

"On his desk, next to his phone."

"He may not get back till late tonight," said Liza. "He's got so many meetings. If you let us in Chan's apartment with your key we'll pick up the ticket. We can pay for it and he can pay us back."

"That's a good neighbor," said Mrs. Merkle. "I'm all through here except for admiring Mr. Hoyt's pigeons. And Mr. Chandler's sparkling window right across the court. Lucky I cleaned it when I did. Otherwise I'd have been embarrassed, looking over at it. I'll meet you over there in two minutes and give you the parking ticket."

"That's one good thing about not having a car," said Mr. Hoyt, turning away from the window to look at Logan. "You never get parking tickets."

"Or rust," agreed Logan, smiling.

Liza and Logan headed for Chan's apartment.

"There is something funny about Chan's having a parking ticket for yesterday, Logan, and you know it."

"We'll see," said Logan.

Mrs. Merkle joined them in a moment in front of Chan's door. She took out a ring of keys. "New key," she said, inserting it in the lock. "Louie brought it over for me when he changed Mr. Chandler's lock this morning. As if life wasn't complicated enough, without changing locks and keys every second."

She walked over to the desk. "Here it is," she said, handing it to Logan. "See, it's for yesterday at two o'clock, just the way I told you."

Logan studied the ticket. Merk was right. It was dated Tuesday, August 4th, two o'clock. The license plate was 054-254.

The rest of the ticket was smeared.

"I know Mr. Chandler will appreciate it if you take care of it," said Mrs. Merkle. "Like I said, unless you pay right away, you pay double." She started to close the door.

"As long as I'm here, I'll just finish cleaning the hall closet. That's where I found the ticket this morning. Right on the closet floor. I've missed my regular bus, anyway, watching those pigeons."

As Logan and Liza walked back into Webb's apartment, Logan said, "There's got to be some easy explanation. Let's call Chan. He said he'd be in meetings all day, and at a dinner meeting tonight, but his secretary can reach him, I bet."

"Do you think he called the police?" asked Liza, frowning.

"We'll soon find out," said Logan, dialing.

"Mr. Chandler's office, Fran Pepper speaking."

Logan cleared his throat and asked the secretary to speak to Mr. Chandler.

"Oh, I can't interrupt him. The best I can do is put a note on his desk. Then maybe he can call you before he goes to his dinner meeting."

Logan left his name and Webb's telephone number. "Please tell him it's important," urged Logan.

He looked at Liza as he hung up. "It's going to be a long wait, Liza."

"I know," said Liza in a small voice. "How could Chan get a parking ticket yesterday? I can't understand it. I guess there are things we don't know." She felt uneasy.

Chapter Six

"Let's have that cheese and crackers and some supper," suggested Liza, jumping up. Maybe if they ate, her uneasy feeling would go away. "Dad said he might be late."

"You talked me into it," said Logan.

They had finished supper when the phone rang. Liza let Logan reach for it. It was Chan.

"This sounds like a stupid question, Chan," said Logan. "But what is the number of your automobile license?"

"It's 78-111," said Chan promptly. "Why do you ask?"

Logan explained about the parking ticket. Chan said slowly, "You say the ticket is for yesterday afternoon, and Mrs. Merkle found it in my apartment this morning?"

"That's right," said Logan.

"Look here, something's wrong," Chan said. "It isn't mine. I didn't get any ticket. Louie brought the plant in, but he doesn't drive a car. No one could have dropped it there. Except—"

"Except the thief," finished Logan excitedly. "He could have dropped it when he came in to steal the money."

Liza sat on the floor and listened intently.

"That's what it looks like, Logan," said Chan.

Logan took a deep breath. "Well, then, it's simple. The police can—"

Chan interrupted quickly. "Logan, I didn't call the police. I couldn't. The police would think that I had made up the story about the money being stolen from my apartment. They would think that I had accepted the bribe and then had hidden the money. I can't prove my story." He paused. "But I don't want you and Liza trying to help. I mean that. I'll think of something. You kids stay out."

"We aren't doing anything," said Logan. "Honest. We just wondered about the parking ticket."

"Do nothing, Logan. I mean it. This could be real trouble."

"Don't worry, Chan," said Logan, hanging up.

Liza looked up at him expectantly.

"Chan doesn't want to call the police. He's afraid it will look as if he accepted Simms and Bowers' bribe. But look. It's not Chan's ticket. How in heck did it get into his apartment—unless the thief dropped it there?"

"That's got to be it," said Liza, her eyes sparkling. "It's our first real clue. We can't let it go. If we find out whose license plate this is, we find out the thief. We've solved the mystery, and how can we be in any danger?"

"But how can we find out who has that license number without the help of the police?" Logan wondered.

"Let's see what we know already," suggested Liza. "We know that the thief came into Chan's apartment sometime after the plant was delivered. Louie brought it in around four o'clock, just before he went home."

Logan continued, "Chan came back in a taxi. He found the money hidden in the plant." He nodded, picturing what had happened. "Chan put the money in the bureau drawer and left. That was around six o'clock. He came back at ten, and the money was gone."

"So we know the money was stolen between six o'clock and ten last night," said Liza.

"And we know that the thief got a parking ticket that afternoon at two," said Logan. "Maybe it fell out of his pocket when he took out a handkerchief or something in Chan's apartment."

"Wait a minute," said Liza. "Didn't Merk say that she found the ticket on the closet floor?"

Logan frowned. "I think she did say that."

"Well, how did it get into the closet?"

Logan rubbed his chin. "Maybe the thief was in the closet, looking for the money," he suggested.

"Or maybe he was hiding," said Liza.

"Hiding," repeated Logan slowly. "I think you've got something."

"The thief had come into the apartment to get the money from the plant," said Liza excitedly. "He heard Chan putting the key in the door. He hid in the closet."

"And heard him putting the money in the bureau drawer," said Logan slowly. "That would explain how the thief knew where Chan hid the money."

"That's it, Logan, that's got to be it! Nobody was looking in the window with binoculars after all. Someone was in the closet, listening."

"So all we need to do is find out who owns the car with this license number," Logan decided.

"The police could do that in a hurry," said Liza. "If only we could call the police."

"Which we can't," Logan reminded her.

"But we've got to do something," Liza complained. "We're so close and yet so far. And every minute we waste just gives more time for the thief to get away."

"I know," Logan agreed. "But if we can't tell the police or Webb or—" Logan suddenly snapped his fingers. "I've got it. I know how we can find out whose car that license number belongs to."

Liza looked at him. "But I don't see how," she began.

"Listen," Logan said. "It's simple. We'll just go down to the Motor Vehicle Department in the morning, and they can run a check on the number. I'll tell them that I had left my car parked somewhere and someone accidentally ran into it."

"They'll believe that all right," Liza interrupted, "but—"

"I'll tell them that whoever ran into the car left his name and his license number, but since it was raining, the name got smeared. I'll explain that I don't want to call my insurance company because the car wasn't hurt badly. I just want to know who to thank for leaving the note. And tell whoever it was not to worry about it."

"Think that will work?" Liza asked doubtfully.

"Only one way to find out," Logan answered. "We'll try it tomorrow morning."

Liza groaned when Logan appeared at the door next morning. "Aren't we awfully early?"

"Come on," Logan urged. "Remember, it was you who said last night that every minute counts.

The Motor Vehicle Department will be open in fifteen minutes."

"All right," Liza said. "Give me three. Dad's just leaving for the library. Then he's going to the airport to pick up your mother. I'll meet you at the car. You might as well go down and make sure it will start."

"Don't let my car hear you say that," Logan laughed as he headed for the elevator.

When Liza came down, Logan was sitting in the car pumping the accelerator. "I told you this car was sensitive," Logan said. "I've flooded it."

"Maybe you've drowned it," suggested Liza. "Anything is possible with this car."

"No problem," Logan assured her.

"We're on our way to find out who the thief is, and your car doesn't work. Are you sure you have the parking ticket?" asked Liza.

"Positive," said Logan, reaching in his pocket. He frowned and took out an envelope. "What's this?" He looked at it and clapped his hand to his head. "I forgot to put these renewal stickers on Mrs. Hinkle's car. I promised I'd do it before this morning for sure. Otherwise she'll be fined. I'll only take a second."

He struggled with the car door. "This I have to fix, for sure."

Logan pushed open the door and ran up the ramp to the second level. In a moment he had found Mrs. Hinkle's little VW. He leaned down to the rear license plate and rubbed a clean spot with his sleeve. Pulling the sticker out of the envelope, he peeled the back off and pressed it to the plate. Then he hurriedly attached the other sticker.

Whistling, he started to walk back along the line of parked cars. Not too many. Most of the tenants of the Brillstone Apartments worked.

Suddenly he stopped and stared: 054-254.

Quickly he reached into his pocket for the parking ticket. He read 054-254.

The same number! This was the car the ticket belonged to. A dark green car, about three years old. Logan walked around it. And then he saw a long scratch from the front to the back. A long scratch? From the front to the back?

It was Keli's car. He was sure of it.

Logan ran along the lines of cars to the ramp and down the ramp to Liza.

"The parking ticket. The license. It's Keli's car!" he said breathlessly.

Liza stared at him. "Keli's car?" She sucked in her breath. "But it couldn't have been Keli. Maybe—"

They looked at each other. "Someone else used

her car. Someone else got the parking ticket," said Logan.

"Thomas," whispered Liza.

"It's got to be Thomas," agreed Logan. "He took her car. And got a parking ticket."

"And put it in his pocket," said Liza. "Then later he must have got into Chan's apartment and lost the parking ticket there."

Logan rubbed his chin. "It was Thomas who called and warned us on the telephone, saying it was not our problem."

Liza blinked quickly. "Poor Keli. Her husband's a thief."

Logan took a deep breath. "Let's go," he said. He started for the stairway door.

"Where to?" asked Liza, running after him.

"To Keli's, where else?" Logan called over his shoulder.

"You mean you're going to tell her what we've found out? About Thomas being a thief?" She caught up to Logan.

"We've got to make sure that Thomas doesn't get away," said Logan.

"But what will we do?" asked Liza breathlessly. "What if he's there? What if he isn't?"

"We'll have to play it by ear," said Logan. "This is it."

Chapter Seven

Keli threw the door open as they knocked. Her face fell as she saw them. "Oh, it's you," she said, turning away. She was wearing a bathrobe. But high heels, Liza noticed. Maybe she was just dressing to go out. Where was Thomas? Were they going out together?

Logan caught Liza's eye and jerked his head toward the door. They followed Keli in and closed the door.

"I'm so worried," said Keli, with a catch in her voice. "I don't know what's happened. He didn't come back last night at all. He left after dinner, and that's the last I've seen of him. When I heard you at the door, I thought it was Thomas."

They'd missed him, thought Logan quickly. He'd already disappeared with the money.

"Tell us," urged Liza, frowning and glancing at Logan.

"Last night we had our dinner. But Thomas was so nervous he hardly ate. And I had all his favorite things." Keli drew a breath and put her glasses on. "Anyway, just as we were finishing, someone came to the door. Thomas took him into the bedroom, and they talked a few minutes. And then Thomas said he had to go out. They left. And he never came back!"

Liza and Logan stared at her. Thomas had run away. With the fifty thousand dollars.

"I just know something awful has happened to him. I know it."

"Who was it who came?" asked Logan.

"I don't know his name. Thomas didn't introduce us. I'd never seen him before."

"But what did he look like?" prompted Liza.

"Little and fat. Bald. He smiled a lot. But I just had a bad feeling about him, about everything."

"Tell us more," urged Logan. They'd have to find out all they could.

"I didn't notice anything else. I only saw him for a few minutes. Oh, he had a gold tooth. I think blue eyes—or were they brown? Oh, I don't remember. I just know that Thomas hasn't come back. Something terrible has happened to him, I just know it."

It was Simms who had come, thought Logan. It was Simms that Thomas had left with. But what did it mean?

"Don't worry, Keli," said Liza. "He'll call you.

He's probably tied up with business or something."

"That's what I've been waiting for," said Keli. Her face crumpled. "I didn't sleep a wink. Maybe he's been in an accident. Maybe he's lying in a hospital ward in the city. Maybe suffering. Maybe I should call the hospitals. Or—"

"Why _don't_ you call the hospitals, Keli?" suggested Liza. "That way you'll feel better. There's no sense in worrying like this."

How long would it be before Keli knew that Thomas had stolen fifty thousand dollars?

"That's a good idea. I'll call the hospitals. Then I'll feel better," said Keli. She pulled open the desk drawer and started to take out the telephone directory. Suddenly she gasped and lifted out a long bulky envelope.

Liza looked over her shoulder. It was a plain envelope addressed in Thomas' big sloppy scrawl: _To Keli_. With shaking fingers, Keli opened it.

The envelope was filled with money.

"I don't understand," breathed Keli. "He doesn't have any money. He wanted to borrow some from me—" She unfolded a sheet of white paper around the bills. She stared at it. Then she handed the scrawled note to Liza. Logan read it with her.

"I'll be in touch Thursday. Wait for my call. This five hundred may help with your bills. Thomas."

Keli kept shaking her head. "I don't understand."

Suddenly she brightened. "But he's all right. He's all right. That's all that matters." She raised her head and smiled at them radiantly.

"That man last night. He probably owed Thomas this money. He paid him, and Thomas wanted me to have it. How could anything be more thoughtful than this?" She held up the packet. "And he needed this money. I know he did. He's been so worried."

Liza glanced at Logan.

Keli went on eagerly, "And he says in the note he's going to call me today. I'll wait right here."

Poor Keli, thought Logan. And poor Chan. Thomas was gone, with the money. All but five hundred dollars. He probably felt guilty. Maybe leaving Keli some of the money made his conscience feel better.

They'd have to call Chan immediately. He had to know that Thomas was the thief. Maybe he'd be willing to call the police now, and the police could take it from there.

"We'll let you get some rest, Keli," said Logan.

"But call us when you hear from Thomas," added Liza. "So we won't worry about you."

"I'm going to have the telephone right next to me while I take my nap," said Keli smiling. "And right next to me while I have a long bubble bath. And right next to me while I have lunch."

A young couple was in the elevator. Logan and Liza didn't speak until they were back at the Webster apartment. Liza sat on the floor, drawing her knees under her chin. "Thomas has gone for good," she said.

"With the money," said Logan gloomily. "What's his connection with Simms?" he asked after a moment, jingling his keys and walking over to the window. "Why did Simms come over to see Thomas? Why did they leave together?"

Liza shook her head. "The briber and the thief. I don't understand it. Let's call Chan."

"At least we can tell him who's the thief," Logan said and reached for the telephone. "It's urgent," he told Chan's secretary.

"Oh, but he's not accepting any phone calls at all. He's in conference," she said. "May I help you?"

"I've got to talk to him," said Logan firmly. "Right away. It's very important."

"But he said he shouldn't be interrupted."

"I don't care. Interrupt him anyway." Logan rubbed his chin. "I'll be at this telephone," and he gave the secretary the number. "Have him call as soon as possible. Please. It's really important." He hung up.

"It's awful to have to wait without doing anything," said Liza, pulling her hair back. "Thomas has vanished into thin air. He might change his name. He might—"

She stood up and walked around the living room nervously.

"It would be easy, if Chan would call the police," said Logan. "Finding Thomas would be their worry."

"But in the meantime, what can we do?" asked Liza.

She walked over to the desk and shifted some papers on the desk. "I feel so helpless," she said. "And I hate being helpless."

Suddenly she wheeled around with a big envelope in her hand.

"Logan. Remember I picked up the wrong folder yesterday? Not Dad's letters. The other ones, the ones Keli'd been typing from the tapes." Logan nodded.

"Well, Keli was typing some things for Thomas, too, remember? Maybe they're in the folder. Maybe there's some clue about where he was going. Some name—some address—that would give us some idea.''

"It's worth a try," said Logan.

Liza rummaged through the big manila envelope. "Here. Three or four letters she typed for a Mrs. Grable. Nothing here of Thomas's. But look, Logan, here are a couple of tapes. Maybe Thomas dictated the letters on here, and she hadn't got around to transcribing them. Or maybe Keli did type them and mailed them, but at least the letters would still be on the tape. Let's listen. Maybe he'll drop a hint about his plans.''

Liza ran into Webb's study. In a moment she was back with the tape recorder. Setting it on the coffee table, she inserted one of the tapes.

She turned on the tape recorder, and a man's voice started speaking, "Dear Mr. Ramsey. Yours of the sixth received. As matters stand—''

"Boring," said Liza after a moment.

"Maybe Thomas's letters come later," suggested Logan. "He'd have used the last part of the tape. Let's keep listening.''

The voice went on, "Dear Mr. Subby. Yours of the tenth received. As you know—''

Liza yawned. "I could write better letters than that,'' she said.

Logan was listening with the edge of his mind to what Liza was saying. But he was listening at the same time to the tape. It droned on. Suddenly—

"Wait a minute!" Logan shouted, leaping to his feet. "Play that again."

"That drivel? Honestly, Logan."

"Didn't you hear what he was saying?"

"Well, no. Frankly, I wasn't listening."

But she turned the tape back. "OK, here are the undying words." And they both heard, "This goes to Mr. Merton Havermill. You've got the address on the sheet. Dear Mert. Sorry to hear there's been so much trouble with shipments. I'll see to it that we get a new shipping clerk pronto. This is not your problem. I repeat, this is not your problem. I'll take care of it."

Liza frowned and shook her head. " 'This is not your problem.' Where have I heard that? 'I repeat this is not—' " She suddenly stopped. "The telephone warning," she whispered. "That's what it is."

Logan nodded. "Listen," he urged her. "There's more."

They stared at the tape recorder as it went on, "Something I do need and fast, more units. I need one hundred and fifty by Thursday. I do mean one hundred and fifty, and I do mean Thursday. We've got to keep on top of things. See you Monday." The voice paused.

"That's what we heard at Keli's," Logan stated. Liza gasped.

The tape was still playing. "Send that right along. Sign my name, the way you've been doing, with my initials underneath, but sign this one Patrick instead of P. Oliphant. Now, to Mr. Orville Harrod. You've got his address. Dear Orville—"

Logan reached over and turned off the tape recorder. "That's what we heard," he repeated. " 'I do mean one hundred and fifty, and I do mean Thursday.' "

"But what does it mean?" asked Liza in a low voice. "It's Thomas, but it isn't Thomas. It's this Mr. Oliphant, whoever he is."

"It isn't Thomas," said Logan slowly. "But it's the voice we heard when we were in Keli's apartment. She played this tape to make us believe Thomas was there—but he wasn't. He wasn't there at all!"

Chapter Eight

Liza raised her eyebrows. "Thomas wasn't there at all. Not in Keli's apartment. We just listened to a tape, right?"

Logan nodded. "This is what we heard. And we believed that it was Thomas."

"But why?" asked Liza, her eyes wide. "Why did Keli try to fool us?"

"I don't know," said Logan slowly. "I just don't know. I'm trying to remember everything that happened. Everything she said. She went into the bedroom to talk to him, remember? But she was just going in to turn on the tape recorder. She wanted us to think that Thomas was talking to her. But he wasn't. No one was. It was just the voice on the machine."

"She must have done it to protect Thomas for some reason," decided Liza. "Maybe to give him an alibi."

"That's got to be it," Logan agreed. "She wanted to be able to prove he was in the apartment when he wasn't."

"But why? What was he *doing* that she didn't want us to find out about?"

Logan rubbed his chin. "Wait a minute. Maybe she wanted to give Thomas time to run away with the money. Maybe he thought we had traced the parking ticket to Keli's car. He'd know that he'd be found out."

"And he asked Keli to make it look as if he was there!" Liza interrupted. "But she may not have known the real reason. Maybe he told her it was just a prank of some kind. A practical joke or something. Because if she had known that he was stealing, she'd have been too upset and angry."

"I wonder," said Logan thoughtfully. "She makes excuses for everything he does. Maybe she'd even make excuses for his stealing money."

"Not Keli," said Liza positively. "But you're right about her making excuses for him. Like his taking the car—taking the keys from her purse without even asking her."

"Or telling her!" added Logan.

"He took her car, and got that parking ticket," said Liza. "That night he let himself into Chan's apartment."

"I wonder how he got the key," said Logan.

"And I wonder how he knew the money would be there," said Liza, frowning.

"Maybe from Simms," suggested Logan. "He and Simms knew each other. It was Simms who came to see Thomas. They left together."

"And Thomas never came back," added Liza.

"He probably never will," sighed Logan. "He may not even know that he lost the parking ticket in Chan's apartment Tuesday night."

Liza looked at the tape recorder. "I just don't understand why Keli tried to fool us," she said. "Tuesday Thomas stole the money. Wednesday, yesterday, we came to Keli's. He wasn't there, but he wanted us to believe he was. So Keli played that tape."

Logan rubbed the back of his neck. "And we were sure it was Thomas. He was gone. And when he came back, they had their anniversary dinner."

"And then Simms came, and Thomas left with him," said Liza, sighing. "We're just going in circles."

Logan walked out to the kitchen and opened the refrigerator. Liza followed him. "See what we've got to eat," she suggested.

"I was," said Logan. "I sure wish Chan would call."

Liza set out two plates and two glasses. "I don't understand Keli's lying to us like that," she said. She glanced at the table and smiled. "If I was with

Michele, I'd set an extra place," she said. "One for Mimzie. And I'd pour milk in her glass, and—"

She stopped and stared at the kitchen table. "Logan, listen. I'd set an extra place for someone who doesn't exist at all," she said slowly. "A make-believe person."

Logan turned around from the refrigerator with some cold cuts and cheese.

"Mmm," he said. "What does all that have to do with Keli and Thomas?"

"I've got a crazy idea, Logan. I haven't even thought it through. But all of a sudden I realized that maybe Thomas is a make-believe person. Like Mimzie, Michele's make-believe friend."

"What are you getting at?" asked Logan, setting the food on the table. "No Thomas? But we saw all his clothes. His briefcase and everything. And we mailed those letters he'd written. And—"

Liza interrupted. Her eyes sparkled with excitement. "Those letters, yes. They helped make us sure that there was a Thomas. But listen, Logan. Last Christmas I sent off a letter for Michele to Santa Claus. She wanted me to send one for Mimzie, too, so I did."

"Michele, Mimzie, Santa Claus—what are you talking about?" asked Logan.

"Don't you see? Keli could have faked everything. The clothes. The *letters*. She faked the voice—why couldn't she have faked everything else?"

Logan jingled the keys in his pocket. "We've never really seen Thomas," he said. "But if she wanted to pretend she had a husband, she certainly wouldn't have invented a slob like Thomas. She'd have at least made us think that he was a rich mining engineer or something. You know, the way some kids always pretend they have glamorous dates out of town so they don't have to admit that no one has asked them to a big dance at school or something. And besides, Thomas was there. I mean, we didn't see him or anything, but I just knew he was there."

"The way I almost feel that Mimzie is there," suggested Liza. "Except Keli was just trying to fool us by making him up."

Suddenly all the pieces began to fit together.

Logan and Liza stared at each other.

"Then it was Keli all along. No Thomas," Logan said finally. "Keli stole the money. And then when she realized she'd lost the parking ticket, she was afraid it would be traced to her car."

"And so she had to pretend that someone else had been driving her car," said Liza excitedly. "Who could it be? Who could she blame for stealing the money? No one. No one except a make-believe husband. That's why she made him so unreliable."

"She made him seem that way so that we could believe he'd steal the money," said Logan. "He could be blamed for the theft. And then he could just disappear. And he could never be traced. Because there isn't such a person." He shook his head. "But how did she do it?"

Liza pulled her hair back excitedly. "Keli had all night after she realized she'd lost the parking ticket, all night to plan what she could do. And she had all morning. All morning to buy the second-hand clothes. And an old briefcase. It's easy to buy initials. And it's easy to fake the luncheon dishes."

"And the special anniversary dinner!" said Logan. "He wasn't going to be there at all."

"And it's easy to let the shower run—I remember hearing it that night when she was getting the dinner ready—and even that sauce she was making. That was just for our benefit. To make us really feel that he existed. That he was real." Liza let her breath out in a long sigh.

"If we hadn't heard the tape we'd still have believed it," added Logan.

"What a plan! What an actress! What a fraud!" said Liza angrily. "Pretending she was upset because he hadn't come home! When he didn't even exist!''

"Leaving part of the money in the drawer was pretty sneaky, too," said Logan. "She's been pretty clever. But maybe not clever enough."

"What now? What if she runs away with the money?" asked Liza.

"She thinks she's succeeded in deceiving everybody," said Logan. "If she ran away now, she'd be proving she was guilty. But she might hide the money."

"If she hasn't already," said Liza. "No one could ever prove Keli is guilty, unless she's got the money." Tossing her hair back, Liza spoke quickly. "Listen. Chan will be calling any minute. You wait here until he does. I'll run down and talk to Keli. I'll think of some excuse. I'll keep her at home until you come. I can be a pretty good actress, too. She'll never know what we know."

"Hurry," urged Logan. "I'll come as soon as I can. As soon as Chan calls. Don't let her leave. Don't let her out of your sight. Don't—"

"Don't worry," Liza called over her shoulder as she left the apartment.

Logan paced back and forth across the living room. "Ring, phone, ring," he muttered. He walked to the window overlooking the entrance to the Brillstone Apartments and stood, tossing his keys from one hand to the other.

Suddenly he stared. Keli was walking out of the apartment building. Liza had missed her!

A large satchel, like a knapsack, swung from Keli's shoulder. The money.

"Sorry, Chan," Logan said under his breath as he sped from Webb's apartment and down the corridor. He reached the elevator and slammed his hand against the button. "Come on," he whispered. He looked up at the floor indicator. The car was up on the twelfth floor. He'd never catch Keli in time if he waited. He ran to the stairway exit and flung open the door. His shoes screeched as he raced around the landing turn, his right arm grabbing the bannister and pulling his long body around. Twisting and turning his weight on the flight of stairs, Logan took three steps at a time. He reached the ground floor and raced past the lobby desk.

"Oh, Logan, I wanted to tell you—" Louie started to say.

"Later, Louie," Logan said breathlessly as he pushed open the big front doors. He stood outside. Where had Keli gone? It had only been a minute or two. She couldn't be out of sight.

He groaned and looked up and down. A taxi

was just waiting to pull out into the street. Taxi. Maybe Keli'd taken a taxi. He ran the length of the driveway to the sidewalk. The taxi pulled out onto the street. Was that passenger Keli? He craned his neck and tried to see into the seat. Someone with a blue cotton hat pulled down. Keli hadn't been wearing a hat.

The taxi driver found a break in the traffic and eased into the street. Keli hadn't been wearing a hat, but had she pulled one on over her hair when she got into the cab?

Quickly Logan checked his pocket for money— he could follow her. Another taxi cruised by.

Just as he was about to hail it, he took one last glance down the street and saw her. She was walking along in the crowd, her short curly hair bouncing, her knapsack swinging.

He took a deep breath and started to follow her, keeping far enough behind so that she wouldn't spot him in the crowd if she turned around. If Keli knew he was following her, she'd make a run for it. She'd hide the money and no one could prove anything. He had to catch her with the money. And get it away from her.

Logan peered over the heads of the other pedestrians, trying to keep her in sight. She crossed the street. The lights changed before Logan reached the corner and the cars surged ahead, blocking her from view.

He couldn't lose her now.

The lights changed and he pushed his way ahead, apologizing to the woman he nearly knocked over and to the old man with a bag of groceries.

Which way?

Elbowing his way through the crowd, he finally saw Keli again and breathed a sigh of relief. She had stopped to look in a store window. Window shopping? Thinking of things she would now be able to buy?

Or was she looking into the window to see if anyone was following her? As he watched, Keli glanced over her shoulder and seemed to look straight at him. Had she seen him?

He ducked behind the two men who were walking ahead of him, talking busily. For the first time in his life he wished he were shorter.

If she had seen him, she'd know. She'd know she'd been found out! She'd be desperate. Chan's words ran through his head: Desperate people do desperate things.

His thoughts raced. He collided with the two men as they slowed their pace, arguing a point. He apologized. The sound of an approaching siren split the air. And when he looked again, Keli was gone.

Logan quickened his pace. She was nowhere to be seen. Across the street? He stood on the curb. His eyes searched the crowds.

The sound of the wailing siren drew near. Cars pulled over to the side of the street. Where had she gone? Into the store? Or was she across the street? He stood on the curb waiting for the screaming siren to pass. An ambulance with flashing red lights was nearing the corner where he stood, squealing its tires as it made the turn.

Suddenly Logan was pushed off balance. A hard push, low in his back. The crowd gasped as he started to fall in the path of the onrushing ambulance. He teetered, trying to catch himself. His arms flailed as he fell forward.

Someone grabbed him, and he fell back on the sidewalk, hard. The ambulance raced past.

Logan lay stunned. A concerned face hovered over him. "Close shave, sonny," someone murmured. Logan shook his head, trying to clear it. A man helped him to his feet.

"Got to watch your step in a city," said a woman's voice. "Those si-reens are enough to make you dizzy."

"You okay, kid?" asked a man in overalls.

"You sure picked a dumb place to fall," a teen-aged girl called as she crossed the street.

But Logan knew he hadn't fallen.

He'd been pushed.

He knew he hadn't imagined it. Someone had tried to push him in front of the speeding ambulance.

It had to be Keli. She must have seen him following her. She must have realized he'd discovered her secret.

Where was she now? He looked quickly up and down the street. She had disappeared. And with her, the money.

His thoughts raced. Keli had seen him, he was sure of it. She knew he was following her. What would she do now? He tried to put himself inside her head. She'd have to hide the money. Hide it before he caught up with her. But where? Where in a busy city could you hide fifty thousand dollars in a hurry?

In a locker. There were lockers in Cronin's Department Store. He and Liza had used those lockers when they were shopping there. Keli had stopped to look in Cronin's window and seen Logan's reflection. Of course, she'd dodge into the store.

He turned quickly. "Hey, watch it," a boy complained.

"Sorry," said Logan over his shoulder. He ran ahead, and pushed through the revolving doors of Cronin's Store. Once inside, Logan walked quickly through the first floor aisles and counters, the stationery department, then perfumes, gloves, purses. The bank of lockers was at the back of the store.

Logan slowed his steps. There were several shoppers at the lockers.

One of them was Keli.

She was fumbling with a small coin purse. The knapsack had disappeared. It must be in a locker. As he moved toward her, she took a coin from the coin purse and started to drop it in the slot.

Logan put his hand on her arm. Keli spun around, her eyes wide behind her big glasses. "Logan!" she gasped. Then she forced a smile. "Why, Logan, what a nice surprise. What are you doing here?"

"Following you," said Logan.

Keli laughed. Her eyes darted sideways. A burly man was putting something in a nearby locker. "Oh, look," she whispered, nodding toward the man. Logan glanced over. Quickly Keli inserted the coin in the slot and started to withdraw the key.

Logan's hand closed over hers.

"Clever you," he said.

"I don't know what you think you're doing," she snapped. She clenched the key in her fist. "I'll make a scene if you try to take it," she said under her breath, smiling.

"Don't think you will," said Logan, forcing her fist open. He took the key.

"Let's stop playing games, Logan," said Keli under her breath. "Simply give the key back to me and I won't make a fuss. Otherwise I'll report you to the management. You're acting *crazy,* absolutely *crazy.* I'll—"

"Call for help. Please do. Send for the police," urged Logan.

Keli bit her lip. "Look, Logan. I have nothing against you. I don't know what's the matter with you. You're acting so strangely. What do you want?"

He nodded toward the locker. Then he turned his back to her. "Your bag," he stated flatly. He inserted the key in the lock and pulled open the door. Let her run, he thought. As long as the money's safe. Chan can have her traced if he wants to. He reached into the locker and took out the big floppy knapsack.

"You're making a fool of yourself," said Keli.

Logan opened the knapsack. He stared. It was empty.

Keli snorted. "And now, if you please, Logan, you go about your business and I'll go about mine—a simple shopping expedition."

Logan stood holding the knapsack. He couldn't have made a mistake. He couldn't.

It was indeed empty.

Wait a minute. If it was empty, why all the fuss? Why had she tried to hide it?

"May I please have my bag?" asked Keli, raising her voice and holding out her hand. Logan gripped it more tightly. He was aware of the burly man turning to stare. He didn't want to make a scene, but—

The knapsack was heavy. Too heavy to be empty. He reached inside and groped. There. He could feel it. A bundle of something hard under the lining. The money.

He glanced at Keli. She was staring at the knapsack, her eyes wide behind the enormous glasses. Then she looked up at Logan and forced a smile. "It is empty, Logan, see?"

Logan smiled back. She wilted. "I don't really feel very well," she said. "Could you get me a drink of water? Or maybe a cup of coffee?"

"Sure," he said. "But no more games. I know all of it."

He put the knapsack securely under his arm.

Keli's eyes darted around the store and then filled with tears.

"Oh, Logan, I'm glad it's over, really glad. It's been a nightmare. Can't we go somewhere and talk?"

"Oh, yes, we'll talk. We'll talk to Chan," said Logan firmly. "We'll take a cab right over to his office now."

Keli hesitated. "But we have to go to my apartment first," she said. "The last five hundred is there. When I see Chan, I want to be able to give him all the money. All of it."

"Okay, first to the Brillstone."

He took her arm and they walked through the aisles toward the revolving door. "After you," said Logan. If she wanted to try to get away, she could. She couldn't get far.

Logan hailed a cab. The driver nodded and turned on the meter. Logan held the knapsack tightly. He half expected Keli to grab it from him.

When they reached Keli's apartment, she sank into a chair and started to cry. "What will become of me?"

"The rest of the money first, please," suggested Logan. Keli darted an angry glance at him. Then she stood up and walked into the bedroom.

In a moment she was back with a large envelope. She watched as Logan counted all the money. Five hundred dollars. Fifty thousand dollars.

"Okay," Logan said. "Now you can cry," he added to himself.

"I never wanted to steal, Logan. I never took anything before now that didn't belong to me. You have to believe me."

"Sure," said Logan. "The devil made you do it. How did it happpen?"

"I was a substitute secretary at Simms and Bowers for two days, typing, switchboard, things like that. Well, I listened in. Eavesdropped. And I heard Mr. Simms and Mr. Bowers planning to bribe Mr. Chandler."

That explained one thing, thought Logan. It explained how she knew about the money in the first place.

Keli went on. "I often hear things. It isn't spying. It's just curiosity. Sometimes my jobs are pretty boring, you know. You can't blame me for just listening in once in a while, can you?"

Logan said nothing. He fingered the keys in his pocket and waited for Keli to continue.

Chapter Nine

Keli looked at Logan and then looked away. "I was tempted, Logan. Oh, how I was tempted! You can understand. I'd never heard of so much money. And I knew Mr. Chandler lived right here in the Brillstone. It was as if it was meant to be. Something told me I was supposed to have that money. It was fate."

She waited for Logan to say something, then she sighed and went on.

"I really thought I could pull it off. And I could have, I could have done it. No one would ever have suspected me! But everything went wrong."

She twisted her hands together and then she looked up brightly.

"I had a key. I'd borrowed the keys from Mrs. Merkle's purse one day when she was cleaning at Webb's apartment. I'd taken up some typing. I got Chan's key copied and had it back in her purse before she missed it."

The key, thought Logan. Another mystery solved.

"How did you know that Simms and Bowers had hidden the money in the plant?" he asked.

"I didn't know that until later. I knew they were going to try to put the money in Chan's car sometime Monday. All the spaces in the garage are marked with names, you know. I checked a couple of times during the day, but that space was always empty. So I thought if they couldn't get the money delivered that way, they'd have to think of another. I guessed they'd try to deliver it the next day, Tuesday."

That explained why Logan and Liza had seen Bowers in the garage. He must have been looking for Chan's car. He'd probably seen him leave in a taxi.

If only Keli would keep talking he could find out the answers to everything. To everything, except what would make anyone—Keli or anyone—steal.

"What did you do?" Logan prompted her.

Keli sighed and stood up. She walked over to the window. "I knew they had to come with the money on Tuesday. The contract was to be awarded Thursday. I stood here and watched. Sure enough. I saw Simms step out of a car with a huge plant. Talk about clever! I waited until I saw him leave. Then I let myself into Mr. Chandler's apartment. Everything would have been fine, but—"

She turned around. She screwed her small face into an angry mask. "I was so close! And no one would have ever known! There was no way anyone could have connected me with the money, or with Simms and Bowers, or with Mr. Chandler! I'd have made it."

"What happened?" asked Logan.

"I read the note on the plant. I didn't see any money, of course. I figured out it must be in the pot somewhere. I started to look. And then I heard a key in the lock. I was terrified. I didn't know what to do. I ran and hid in the closet."

Logan nodded.

"I heard Chan trying to get Simms and Bowers. And I heard him hiding the money in the bedroom. And I heard him leaving. Then I got the money," said Keli bitterly. "It was going to work! But—" She bit her lip.

"When did you realize you'd left the parking ticket in the closet?" asked Logan.

"About an hour later, at least. I had that whole hour to believe I'd made it. I counted the money. I looked at it, I handled it, I kissed it! I was going to put it in a bank in another city, leave it there a couple of months. Then—" She blinked. "When I realized I'd lost the parking ticket, I knew I'd have to get it back. I crept down the stairs. I started to let myself in. But you were there!"

It had been Keli that night. If only he had caught up with her then!

Keli paced around the living room nervously. "I had the money. But now that stupid parking ticket. My car." She tilted her head and looked at Logan. The light from the windows reflected in her big glasses. Logan couldn't see her eyes, but he could see her tight smile.

"My car, Logan, yes. Someone would soon realize that my license was the one on the parking ticket. The parking ticket could be traced to my car."

She hugged herself. "It could be traced to my car—but not to me! Had *I* been driving it? Had I been the one to get the parking ticket? Of course not. I could invent a husband. I could invent a guilty, irresponsible husband. He had stolen the money. Not me! And no one would ever be able to track him down. Not if they looked a thousand years."

"That was fast thinking," said Logan grudgingly. "So you invented him that night."

"I stayed up all night, planning, figuring out how I could do it. I'd need clothes. That was easy. But I had to do better than that. I had to make you and Liza and everyone believe that he was a real live person. I had to make up a personality for him. I had to make him just strange enough so that you could believe he might be a crook if you found out about the parking ticket and traced it to my car."

Her eyes sparkled behind the huge glasses. "I made up everything. Everything. Even handwriting for him. I wrote with my left hand. And I played the tapes I had over and over, trying to find a phrase here or there that I could use. Oh, Logan, it was perfect!" She clapped her hands.

"Almost," said Logan under his breath.

Keli spoke proudly. "The next morning I bought some clothes. There's a seconds store over on Mason Drive. I even saw a briefcase while I was there. I bought it. The initials were a special touch, I thought, T.O.M. I picked them up in a drugstore."

"You thought of everything," said Logan dryly.

"Yes," said Keli coldly. "Everything but you."

"You really had us fooled," admitted Logan.

Keli turned quickly, her glasses glinting. "Us?" she asked. "Liza knows about me, of course?"

Something made Logan shake his head. He had to keep Liza out of this. "Oh, Liza doesn't know yet. I'll explain everything to her later."

He stood up. "Let's go to Chan's now, Keli. You can tell him everything you've told me. As long as he has all the money, he can decide what he wants to do about prosecuting Simms and Bowers for bribery. And you for theft. Maybe he'll understand."

"Maybe he'll be kind," said Keli. "Just a second. I'll get my purse. And I've got to freshen up my face."

In a few minutes she came back from the bedroom with a black purse. Logan picked up the knapsack.

"Oh, Logan, it's true what I said. I've never done anything wrong before. Never. But I just couldn't help myself. Mr. Chandler will understand, surely."

"We'll see," said Logan. They started out of the apartment. "As long as this is your first time—"

"And my last," Keli assured him, smiling eagerly and taking his arm. "Really, Logan, I wouldn't go through all that again for anything in the world. All that worry, all that suspense."

They stood at the elevator.

"Logan," she said softly. "Let's go right to your car. I don't want to take a cab. I couldn't walk through that lobby, I just couldn't. I'd be too ashamed."

"But no one knows but me," said Logan.

"I just couldn't walk through there anyway," said Keli. "But it's true what you say. No one knows." Keli's eyes sparkled. They stepped into the elevator. They took the elevator to the garage.

Keli shivered. "I've got a sweater in my car," she said, as they walked over to Logan's car. "Do you mind if I get it?"

"That's okay," said Logan. It flashed through his mind that she might try to run. Well, even if she escaped from him now, she couldn't get too far. And Chan would have the money. He could have her arrested if he wanted to.

Keli ran up the ramp to her car, swinging her black purse. Logan put the key in the lock of his front door. It didn't work. He tried again. He'd have to fix that door handle this weekend for sure. He hung Keli's knapsack around his shoulders and took the handle in both hands.

And then the entire garage was plunged into darkness. The fuse box, thought Logan quickly.

He heard an engine starting up. Keli? Was she going to try to run away after all?

Suddenly headlights from the ramp above blinded him. He lifted his arm to shield his eyes. The lights aimed straight at him as the car picked up speed. He stared in horror as the car hurtled toward him. He was paralyzed with fear.

Suddenly Logan threw himself out of the path of the onrushing car. The earsplitting sounds of splintering glass and grating metal against metal echoed through the garage. He hit the concrete. Stunned, he lay there a moment, his breath coming in short gasps. His head throbbed. A dagger of pain shot through his ankle and he winced. The sudden silence seemed to him as loud as the sound of the crash. He lay on the cement, tense and waiting.

And then he heard a car door opening. His eyes shot to Keli's car, rammed against his own. One of her headlights had been smashed. The other cast strange misshapen shadows through the dark garage.

He saw her step out of her car. The light hit her glasses. She looked as if she was wearing a mask.

Something heavy and metallic dropped on the cement. It echoed hollowly through the garage.

Logan's eyes widened in shocked disbelief. A gun.

Summoning all his strength, he dragged himself behind a car. He pushed the knapsack out of sight behind a wheel. He'd have to run. He had to get away from Keli—and her gun.

He tried to sit up, and a wave of sickness hit him. Where could he hide?

He forced himself to his feet and crouched behind the car, his heart pounding. Where was she? He strained his ears. No sound. And then he heard her. She was walking toward him.

He spun around, his eyes wildly searching for a hiding place. He ran, limping, toward a large pillar. He reached the post and drew himself behind it, afraid to breathe. The huge shadows of the silent cars loomed on the walls. Logan's heart pounded madly in his ears. He was afraid its sound would give away his hiding place.

He listened and waited. Nothing. She was waiting, too, listening for him. The sickness he had felt before returned, and he broke out in a cold sweat.

Then he heard broken glass crunch under her approaching steps. The eerie light from the single unbroken headlight threw her shadow to the ceiling in a long ragged patch. Suddenly her voice called.

"Logan? Logan, I'm so sorry about your car. My accelerator stuck. I couldn't stop. Are you all right?"

Logan's thoughts screamed inside his head. Where could he hide? How could he hope to outrun a gun? Taking a shuddering breath, he made a quick dash away from the pillar and toward another car. He dodged behind it, shaking.

"Logan? You're not angry with me, are you? I really feel terrible about your car. It was an accident. I'll make it up to you. I'll pay for it."

Her shadow, huge and distorted, moved against the garage wall.

Logan inched himself lower and lower until he was able to peer under the car. He was staring directly at her shoes, only a stone's throw away. He held his breath and waited. Keli stood motionless. She didn't know where he was. Or did she? The only sound in the garage was her breathing. If only he could make it to the stairway door, he'd be safe. He held himself rigid, not daring to blink an eye. His ankle throbbed.

She started to walk slowly toward the car he was hiding behind.

Suddenly he lost his balance, bumping against the car. He cursed his ankle as he lunged painfully from his crouched position. Ducking behind cars, turning and twisting, he limped toward the door to the stairway. His own shadow, huge and grotesque, loomed threateningly. It was like every bad dream he'd ever had, trying to run from something but running in slow motion, running through sand. He gasped with pain and fear as he neared the stairway door.

And suddenly Keli was in front of him, her

hands hidden in her pockets, the black bag slung over her shoulder.

Logan stood paralyzed. There was nowhere else to run. A movement behind Keli jerked Logan's gaze away from her face.

"Liza!" cried Logan. "Go back! Get out!"

Keli's short, high-pitched laugh echoed through the garage. "I've heard that trick before, Logan," she said. "You want me to turn around in surprise and you'll grab me, right? Well, I don't fall for cheap stunts."

In a flash, Liza rushed from the stairway door and grabbed Keli, falling with her. Where was the gun? Logan groped around on the floor for it.

"Run, Liza," he urged hoarsely, trying to help her to her feet. Keli sat up.

"What on earth do you two think you're doing?" she asked. "And why did you knock me down, Liza?"

"Don't try double-talk, Keli," said Logan angrily. His heart was pounding and his head ached. The danger was not over.

He turned to Liza. "She deliberately ran her car into mine. I jumped clear. But just in time."

Liza gasped. "But—" she started to say and stared from Logan to Keli.

"Oh, Logan," Keli interrupted. "I told you it

was an accident. My accelerator jammed, that's all. I'm sorry about the car. Aren't you going to help me up?''

Logan helped Keli to her feet.

"Really, I was worried for fear I'd hurt you, Logan," she said. "And then you were so silly. You ran away! As if you were afraid of me." She laughed. "As if I was after you with a gun or something!"

Suddenly she thrust a gun at Logan. Instinctively he recoiled.

"Look! It's empty," she said. "I just carry it for protection!" She started to shake with sobs.

"I've seen that trick before, Keli," Logan said slowly. "I don't fall for cheap stunts."

Keli's hunched form straightened and she looked angrily at Logan. Behind her glasses her eyes were narrow and dry. "Oh, if I'd been lucky—" she whispered.

"What on earth is happening?" asked Liza. "I came looking for you and—"

"No problem," said Logan. He looked through the dark shadows to the two cars, locked together in a strange, silent battle. "I'll get someone over here to rescue the cars. And I'll fix that little problem with the lights. A fuse somehow got itself unscrewed."

He knelt down and reached for the knapsack under a nearby car. "Next stop, Chan's office, in a taxi," announced Logan. "We'll have a lot to tell him." He patted the knapsack under his arm.

Keli shrugged. "We'll see who he believes," she said.

Chapter Ten

Logan and Liza would never forget any part of that day. It seemed years instead of hours until they were finally sitting in Webb's apartment with Webb and Jenny. Chan was to join them later.

"You had a lot more fun and excitement here at the Brillstone than I had in Bermuda," said Jenny smiling.

"Excitement, yes. Fun, no," said Logan, rubbing his ankle. "Besides, my perfectly good car is now a piece of junk."

"It always was," said Liza. "But now you admit it."

"Peace," laughed Logan.

"Tell me everything," urged Jenny.

"We'll leave out the scary parts," said Logan.

"But they're the best," Liza objected.

"Look who's talking," said Logan. "Remember how you jumped when the lights went out in the garage on Monday?"

"Start at the beginning," said Jenny. "I want to hear every single thing."

"That *was* the beginning, in a way," said Liza, piling her hair on top of her head.

"Talk away," said Webb. "Our dinner is safely in the oven. When we're ready for it, it will be ready for us."

"I'd rather talk than eat," said Liza. "Wouldn't you, Logan?"

"No. But talking will do for now."

"Hurry and tell me all," Jenny insisted.

Logan and Liza talked quickly. Webb and Jenny asked questions from time to time.

"The parking ticket was your only clue, then?" asked Jenny after a while. "Until you heard the tape?"

"Well, there were lots of red herrings, leads that confused us," confessed Liza. "We thought at first someone might have looked over at Chan's apartment with binoculars and seen him hiding the money. But that wasn't true."

"One thing I can't figure out," said Liza. "Why did Keli tell us about the scratch on her car? It just made it easier for us to know it was hers."

"She told us about the scratch before she got the parking ticket she dropped at Chan's apartment," Logan explained.

"And those envelopes you mailed?" asked Jenny. "What were they?"

"I asked about that," said Logan. "The envelopes were just stuffed with blank sheets of paper. She'd made up all the names and everything else. It was just one more trick to make Thomas seem real to us."

"And to make him seem pretty shifty and unreliable," added Webb.

Jenny spoke up. "Keli was clever enough, all right, making up all those things so that you would believe he existed. She even gave him a personality. But what if Chan had gone to the police? They could have found out that there were no records of a Thomas O. Morrison at all. No tax records, no job records, no marriage records. The police could have learned in a jiffy that Keli had made him up."

"I asked her about that, too, on the way to Chan's office," said Logan. "She was ready for that. She was going to make it clear that he had lied to her about everything—about his name, his background, everything. Even the police would have felt sorry for her, thinking he had fooled her even about their getting married."

"What about the lights going out in the garage just before Keli tried to ram you with her car?" asked Webb.

"She'd been in the garage on Monday. She'd

seen Bowers there. One of the maintenance men had blown a fuse. She remembered that the fuse box was on the same level with her car."

"She has a mind like a sponge," said Webb. "She absorbs everything. That's what made her so efficient." He sighed. "I'll miss her. She was a good secretary."

"I'll help, Dad," said Liza.

"There's something else I've been wondering about," said Webb, rubbing his pipe. "Why did Keli run when she did? Not sooner, not later?"

"Well, we talked to her about it on the way to Chan's," said Liza. "She was anxious to tell us all she could, to get on our good side. In the first place, she decided that if Thomas was suspected, someone would want to look around her apartment. And in the second place, she realized that she had the envelope with Webb's letters. She assumed—correctly, of course—that Liza had taken the wrong envelope. With the tapes with Thomas's 'voice'. She was afraid Webb might play one by accident and hear the telephone voice say, 'This is not your problem.' "

"Hiding the money in the department store locker was the fastest and safest thing she could think of on the spur of the moment," added Logan. "She had to get rid of it before I caught up with her.

Otherwise there would be no proof ever that she had been the thief."

"What about her saying that Simms had come to see Thomas? What was that about?" asked Webb.

"Just to confuse things," explained Logan. "She knew what Simms and Bowers both looked like from the day or two she had worked there. If anyone had asked Simms about Thomas, of course he'd have denied knowing him. But no one would have believed him."

"That's the thing about lying," said Jenny. "No one *ever* believes you, even when you're telling the truth."

"I don't know how Keli could have been so convincing," said Liza, shaking her head. "I mean, she seemed so upset when she said Thomas hadn't come back all night, and—"

Jenny tilted her head. "The old red eye trick," she explained. "I've used it myself when I wanted to get my way. Just wash your face with soap and water and let a little soapsuds get in your eyes. It works every time."

Webb smiled at her. "I'll remember that, Jenny," he said.

At that moment there was a knock at the door. It was Chan.

"Sorry I'm late," he smiled, "but I've had a rather hectic week. To say nothing of the last couple of hours. Jenny, you're looking lovely as ever." He winked at Liza and Logan. "No point in asking how you two spent the afternoon. All I can say is 'thanks,' and that I've been taught a good lesson."

All eyes focused on Chan as he settled himself into a chair. "If I had called the police in the first place—as my better judgment told me to do—no lives would have been endangered. I guess I was just thinking of myself and my reputation."

Logan spoke up. "Actually, it was very exciting and it sure beat doing errands. Anyway, you told us not to become involved. It wasn't your fault. We were just glad to help."

"Which brings me to another point," Chan said, folding his hands. "Now, I'd like to do something for you. I've been thinking of getting another car. Since your car is no longer very useful, I'd like to give you my Ford."

Logan's eyes widened. "No, Chan, I couldn't, after all—"

Chan raised his hand. "Let's hear no more about it. As you know, it's been in the shop all week. My mechanic tells me it's getting too old for all the trips I take it on, but it's great around town.

And the Brillstone Apartments couldn't survive without its errand people—errand persons. Look at it as a community service."

"Well, as long as you put it that way," Logan grinned, "how can I refuse? It'll keep Liza and me out of trouble, and as long as the doors work, Liza won't mind doing even more errands."

Liza winked at him. "I'd like to say I'll miss your old car, but I can't. And there's a new tenant moving in, so we'll be plenty busy."

Chan handed the keys to Logan. Logan started to get out of his chair. "Chan, do you mind if—"

But Webb interrupted him. "We can all look at the car later. Right now we've got a dinner to settle down to."

Logan grinned. "Food. Sometimes it's hard making decisions."

About the Authors □ Must members of a writing team live near each other? That may be necessary for others, but the Heides, a mother-and-daughter team, prove it's not so for them. Florence Parry Heide, whose home is in Kenosha, Wisconsin, and Roxanne, who lives in Cheyenne, Wyoming, start a book with a series of get-togethers, perhaps at a family lakeside cottage or a Colorado resort. They then work by mail and telephone until the time comes to put the finishing touches to the manuscript. Another meeting, and a new story is ready.

Florence Heide brings versatility and enthusiasm to all she does. She's written lyrics for songs, picture books (including the popular *The Shrinking of Treehorn*), short novels for teen readers, stories for reading programs, and of course many popular mysteries. Roxanne has produced textbook material and collaborated on five mysteries in the Spotlight series published by Albert Whitman.

Knowing her stories are being read and enjoyed by children gives Florence Heide a special sense of accomplishment. When the votes by schoolchildren in grades four through eight in Wisconsin schools were tabulated, Florence Heide became the winner of the Golden Archer Award for 1977. Among her titles mentioned time and again were *Mystery at MacAdoo Zoo* and *Mystery of the Bewitched Bookmobile*.